NIGHT OF MATCHSTICKS

PART TWO OF THE HOUSE OF MATCHSTICKS SERIES

ELISA DOWNING

ISBN: 978-1-7773305-6-9 (Electronic Book)

ISBN: 978-1-7773305-5-2 (Paperback)

ISBN: 978-1-7773305-7-6 (Hardcover)

Cover Art by Merilliza Chan

First edition, 2021

For content warnings, visit Elisa's website at elisadowning.com/content-warnings.

For Wendy
Mother, listener, healer.

BENEMOURNE
(East Side)
FORT UPPER
CASRET ACADEMY
LOWER VILLAGE
THE MILL
AR
N
W
E
S
THE SHUTE
SUNREST

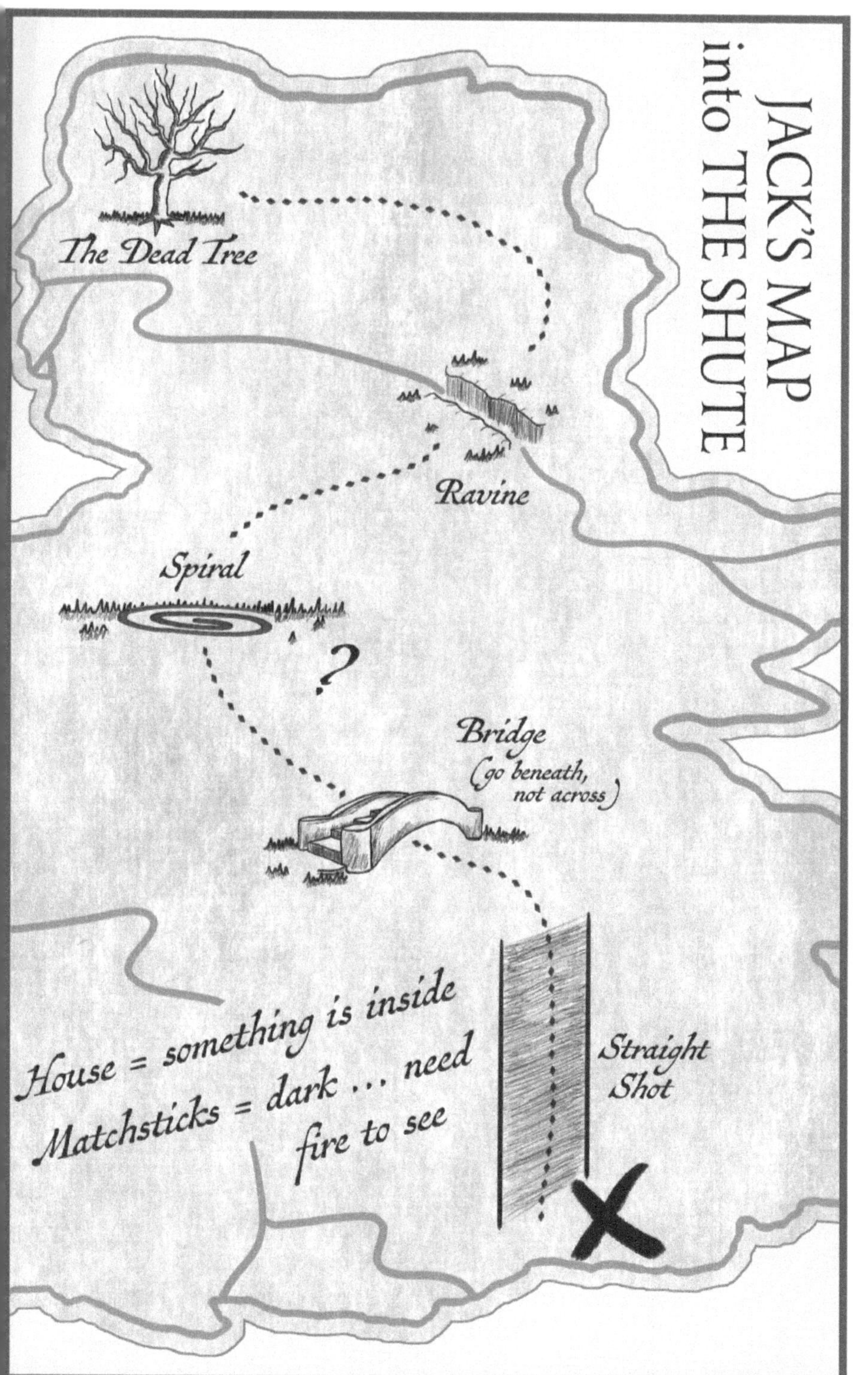
JACK'S MAP
into THE SHUTE
The Dead Tree
Ravine
Spiral
?
Bridge
(go beneath,
not across)
House = something is inside
Matchsticks = dark ... need
fire to see
Straight
Shot

TABLE OF CONTENTS

PRONUNCIATION GUIDE

Adrudian → a-DREW-dee-an
Agustin → Ah-GUST-in
Caladrius → cal-AH-dree-us
Fael → FYE-ell
Faraday → fair-AH-day
Isaline → ee-SAH-leen
Jame → JAY-m
Minna → MEEN-ah
Nalissa - nah-LISS-ah
Neave → NEEV
Purpesia → perp-EZ-ee-ah
Rhody → RO-dee
Shute → SHOOT

Night of Matchsticks

PART TWO OF THE HOUSE OF MATCHSTICKS SERIES

1

THE MESSAGE

JACK

Jack Fael couldn't stop thinking about the monster Neave had thrown out the window.

The window had been high, ten stories up the dormitory of Casret Watch Academy, and the monster had been fleshy. A man-snake—or maybe more *worm* than snake. Nothing that doughy survived a fall from ten stories.

Still, when they had ushered the monster's shocked victim from her building and into the rain, Casret's grassy square had been empty. A spatter of broken glass, nothing else. Nothing where *something* should have been.

The storm had let up by the time Jack, Neave, and their cargo—Nalissa, a young spy for the Quandary of Thieves—reached the outskirts of Fort Upper. Jack was soaked. Shivering, he patted the drenched sleeve of his jacket closer to his forearm. The burns he'd sustained working at Ar's Adrudian mill calmed against the cool, wet fabric. Jack himself longed for a drink of something a little stiffer than rainwater.

"This way," Neave said. She brightened the gravel path with the flashlight from her weapons belt.

The trail from Casret Academy to Fort Upper was forested and barely lit. The lampposts lining the road needed a change of Adrudian. Ore had either become too expensive in these parts or there hadn't been any to replace the old, dim rocks. Jack marked the shortage in his notebook with a damp pencil; his research habits had lingered even after he'd quit Treasurehunting. He wrote blindly as they walked, shadowy trees rising on either side of the road like small mountains.

As they entered the gates of Fort Upper, the clouds above dissipated and faint early morning stars shone through. Neave was up ahead with her flashlight. Jack looked over his shoulder at the young Quandary spy, bringing up the rear of their procession. The soles of her boots dragged across the path, and umber curls were plastered to her face with rain. She'd slung the trident she had insisted on stealing over her back—incorrectly. It would get caught behind her if she tried to unsling it. Casret Academy had a poor reputation for education, but the oversight surprised Jack nonetheless. King Faraday clearly didn't care about his City Watch, not when he had fleets of clockwork soldiers to do his bidding.

"Keep up," Jack called back to the spy, but her boot-dragging continued.

Fort Upper was a small, bustling city, the body of which was wide streets, marbled buildings, and waves of people hurrying to catch their trains, kicking up mud in their wake. Neave put away her flashlight, brushed at the tops of her purple boots, and brandished a train ticket in front of her like a shield. She pushed her way through the crowds with Jack and the girl trailing behind.

Rounding a corner, Jack was forced up against the tall iron wheel of a carriage. A heavy trunk teetered on the carriage's roof before slipping and nearly flattening Jack's toe. The driver looked down his mustache at Jack, eyes narrowed.

"Watch where you're going, Blueveins."

Jack took a wide step over the fallen trunk and kept on.

Stands and vendors crowded the steps at the entrance of Upper Train Station, selling roasted roots, vegetables, and other forage from the surrounding forests. An acrid cocktail of smoke, grease, and burning Adrudian ore filled Jack's lungs and sickened his stomach. He shielded his eyes from the new sun and followed Neave as she climbed the marble staircase.

Inside the station, they stopped inside a huge, cathedral-like room with vaulted windows and enormous, ticking clocks lining the walls. The crowd buffeted them in all directions. Jack imagined himself a porcupine with quills that stuck into anyone who came near.

"Right on time," Neave said, smiling at the Quandary girl. The spy didn't return her smile, just swallowed and looked nervous, her dark brows twitching. "Our train should be boarding."

The three of them cut left and descended a long, wide flight of stairs under a cream-colored archway. The sharp tang of burning Adrudian stung Jack's nose. It coated his tongue and dried his mouth, its smell as tangible as chewing on chalk.

Beyond the archway, the train platform was cavernous and bright, lit by natural light filtering from the cloudy glass ceiling above them. Huge tunnel openings at either side of the tracks led into darkness. Crowds of people pushed toward the train.

Jack stepped onto the platform and grimaced as his foot sunk into a puddle of copper-colored, powdery sludge. Adrudian Milk, the gooey byproduct created when Adrudian ore was burned for energy. He lifted his boot and shook it off, but it was no use—Milk was everywhere, pools of it dotting the platform. Attendants busied themselves mopping it up in the spaces between jostling people.

"Engine overflow," a raspy voice said to his left. "Tell your future for three pieces of silver."

Jack turned. Through the bodies rushing to catch the train, he saw an old woman slumped against the wall, draped in a dark, scratchy-looking cloak. A stand had been set up next to her, a disc of iron with a small hole in its center supported on three long legs. Her face was a nest of blue, climbing veins. She had one pale, bony hand outstretched and a keen eye gazing at him.

He glanced toward the train. Neave and the girl had gone ahead of him; they stood at the edge of a mass of people waiting to funnel into the cars. The girl studied her ticket while Neave checked her pockets for something. They wouldn't miss him for a moment or two, and he'd give a thousand pieces of silver for some blessed time alone.

Jack walked toward the woman. She had no eyebrows, but the skin where they should have been rose as he approached.

"Oh, dear." She retracted her hand. It disappeared into the folds of her cloak. "You don't need me to tell your future, do you, Drinker?"

Jack grunted. He slid a hand into the damp pocket of his coat, fishing for the coins he'd brought. "Three pieces, you said?"

The Drinker considered him, watery eyes glinting within their puffy sockets. "Are you Parched?"

"Don't be foolish." Jack counted out the pieces of silver in his hand. They gleamed against his calloused skin. "Parched people don't exist. No one stops Drinking." He held out the money, but the Drinker just stared at him, wrinkling her smooth brow. He sighed. "You can take it or not."

Her eyes flashed. She took the money from his palm. Jack closed his fingers, and she smiled through a mouthful of teeth.

"Well," she said. "Perhaps I'll tell you what you don't already know."

Humming to herself, the Drinker rummaged under a fold in her cloak. Jack watched her, rubbing his fingers over the back of his aching neck. Cameron Agustin, Treasurehunting's biggest celebrity and professional thorn in Jack's side, had booked him a room at an inn before sending him on this trip. Jack had slept in a straw bed for rent instead. The bed had been uncomfortable as a pile of rocks, but it was better than spending two days befriending Neave at the inn, as Cameron must have intended. Jack wasn't much for friends.

The Drinker rummaged until she retrieved a tarnished metal cup. Jack took it from her outstretched hand. It was heavy, well-used.

"Fill it," the Drinker said.

She reached back into her cloak and pulled out a small, bright piece of Adrudian ore. It was orange and rutted, the same ore Jack shoveled and cooked at Ar's Adrudian mill. His eyes followed the ore's glow as the Drinker placed it onto the metal stand.

"You light the match." She handed him a long matchstick. "Let's make sure the vision belongs to you."

Jack bent and struck the match on the stand's leg. He handed it to the Drinker, and she held it to the Adrudian.

Flickering, the flame encompassed the rock of ore, engulfing its rough surface like a bright mouth closing. Adrudian Milk oozed and ran toward the hole at the center of the metal disc.

Jack's senses contracted, the sounds of voices on the platform muffling. He leaned and caught the dripping Adrudian Milk in the metal cup. The smell prickled the insides of his nostrils. When the ore had burned away, the woman took the cup from Jack, brought it to her lips, and drank the contents.

Nothing happened for a few seconds. Having experienced them himself, Jack thought of these seconds as a resting period, a moment sitting on the edge of a cliff before pitching into the abyss below. The Drinker stared, expressionless. She let the hand holding the metal cup fall. Then a cloudy white film spread across her eyes, and Jack went still.

"*I see a dark cave in the Earth.*" The Drinker's voice was sharp and cold-clear, like melting ice. "*I see a wall of stone.*"

Jack folded his arms, pressing them tight to his chest.

"*Wait* ..." The Drinker paused. She swallowed, smacking her lips. "*There's someone behind the wall.*"

Jack sighed, letting his arms relax. Drinking Adrudian was a game of chance. Having a full, comprehensible vision of the future or past was rare; in Jack's case, most visions were just flashes of arbitrary images. Still, the small chance of having a meaningful vision kept gullible travelers paying and Drinkers Drinking. Jack himself had been one of the desperate ones, trying and failing to use Adrudian Milk to uncover the lost memory of his last Treasure-hunting expedition.

"*She's staring at you. From behind the wall.*" The Drinker's hand clutched the cloak covering her chest. Jack was only half-listening now, his eyes wandering over the crowd and toward the train. "*She has a message for you.*" The Drinker's voice lowered. "*From the House of Matchsticks.*"

Jack whipped his head so fast his neck cramped. "What?"

The Drinker mumbled something too quiet to make out, eyelids fluttering. Jack's stomach flipped. Was he hearing things? She couldn't have said *House of Matchsticks*, the name of the very place about which Jack had been trying to recover memories. The place where he and Cameron had almost died trying to find. He rifled around in his jacket, looking for his notebook.

"What did you say?" he asked, flipping to a blank page with frantic fingers. "Did you say *House of Matchsticks*?"

The Drinker had started to tremble. She opened her mouth and her jaw opened, no sound coming out. Jack's heartbeat stuttered. She was losing it, shifting into another vision. He abandoned his notebook and kneeled in front of her.

"Tell me." Before he could stop himself, Jack clenched

the front of the Drinker's scratchy cloak in his hands. He shook her. "Tell me what you see."

The Drinker's head sagged to the side, neck limp, teeth chattering. Jack leaned until they were face-to-face. She was light, a pile of bones beneath the cloak. Someday soon, this Drinker would take her last sip of Adrudian Milk, the poison having finally overcome her blood and body.

But not today.

"Tell me, don't lose it." Outside of himself, Jack registered that people on the platform had stopped to stare. He shook the Drinker again, hard enough to make her head wobble. "What is the message? Tell me! *Tell me!*"

A boot connected with Jack's side. The Drinker's cloak slipped from his fingers, and he went sprawling on the ground, landing on his shoulder. The impact pulled a groan from his mouth. He pressed his eyes shut, then opened them to find a City Watchman standing over him, his black coat swallowing the dawn light.

"What do you think you're doing?" the Watchman said. His voice was tinny, like he was speaking out of his nostrils. He reached out with the toe of his boot and pushed Jack over onto his back. "You feeling a little thirsty, Blueveins?"

Jack tried to speak, but couldn't get a sound out beneath his heaving lungs. The Watchman crouched and pushed a clump of Jack's hair from his face.

"It's supposed to be my day off," he said.

Jack turned his head and saw two other Watch, a man and a woman, hauling the Drinker off the platform. The Drinker's eyes were pure white. She seemed to be staring at him.

"I'm sorry," Jack wheezed, calling after her. Her legs and cloak disappeared up the steps, trailing on the marble. "I'm sorry—I didn't mean to—"

The Watchman reached out and clutched Jack's cheeks between his thumb and middle finger. His gloves were blinding ivory, almost as white as his skin. "No, no, no," he said, and pinched, making Jack's lips pucker and the insides of his cheeks crush against his teeth. "She's with them now. And let me make something clear." He came close, glaring into Jack's eyes. "There's only one reason you're not with me, and that's the two people back there who seem to have a train ticket for you."

Faces swam into focus over the Watchman's shoulder. Neave, red and fuming, being held by the arm of another Watch, and the Quandary girl, who looked so alarmed Jack thought she might faint. The Watchman smiled. The cologne he wore—some oversweet flower—wafted into Jack's face.

"Lucky for me," he said, so low only Jack could hear, "I've got a train ticket, too. Going to be a long ride. My name's Donborough, and I'll be looking for you, Blueveins."

Donborough held up Jack's notebook—the only place where Jack had been chronicling his research, the Adrudian shortage at the mill, his visions, *everything*—and tucked it into his black coat. He stood and walked off.

Jack's face burned as he struggled to sit, one hand clutching his throbbing shoulder. "Wait—my notebook —*wait!*" he said, but the eyes of the crowd on the platform stopped him.

The Watchman in front of Neave retracted his arm and she rushed to Jack, holding out a hand to help him up. He ignored it and got to his feet himself, brushing at his clothes.

"What are you all looking at?" Neave said to the crowd. "The train is boarding, isn't it?"

The gawkers dispersed. Jack scanned for Donborough. The crowd had started back toward the train, but Jack caught a glimpse of thin hair and snow-white gloves cutting through the sea of people like a shark. Donborough boarded the train at the far end of the platform.

Neave adjusted her weapons belt, catching the eye of the Quandary girl hovering at the edge of the crowd.

"Come on," Neave said, gesturing to them both. "We'll go to the other side."

NEAVE PICKED an alcove of seats in a near-empty car at the back of the train, away from the eyes of other travelers. She piled their things into one of the luggage compartments and pulled down the smooth shade on the window.

The light dimmed. Jack sank into his seat and rubbed his hands over his face, trying to ignore his crawling skin.

"I think we could all use some sleep," Neave said. She hadn't looked at him since they'd come in off the platform. She might have been angry, but Jack suspected that she was sorry for him, which was worse. "If you lay like that, Nalissa, you'll wake up with a headache."

The Quandary girl had stretched out so her head was against the wall of the train. Neave tucked her braid into the inside of her waistcoat and lay down the opposite way. "That wall's going to shake the whole journey," she said, "and turn your brain to stew by the time we get there."

The girl changed her position, mirroring Neave and putting her feet against the wall. Jack watched as she pulled her maroon overcoat across her body like a blanket. She had never been on a train before, that was obvious enough—did Cameron really plan to bring this girl on their expedition into the mines?

"And you," Neave continued, pointing at Jack, "you stay out of trouble. Cameron would kill me if we arrived with you on a stretcher."

Jack frowned at her. "You're not my babysitter."

"Hardly." To Jack's surprise, she flashed him a warm smile before closing her eyes and settling her head back against the edge of the seat. "But I can see why he likes you."

Jack lay awake for a long time after the train rumbled out of the station. The rough green fabric of the seats stuck to his drying coat, forcing him to peel himself away every time he moved. Next to him, Neave had fallen asleep. The thin line of light coming in under the blinds slid across her face, making shadows above her heavy lashes.

The Quandary girl spent a few moments peeking under the blinds, watching as the train emerged from the tunnel and rose over the forest at Casret Academy. The sun warmed the beige tones in her features, but underneath was still an anxious gray. Finally, she turned to face the back of the seat, huddling up under her coat. Before long, her breathing deepened and she was asleep, too.

Jack's mind wouldn't let him sleep. The Drinker's vision on the platform rolled around in his head like a boulder on the deck of a tossing ship.

She has a message for you.

From the House of Matchsticks.

A message—what kind of message? And what if he could *receive* that message? Soon?

Now?

The possibility set his heart racing. Lying still was impossible. He sat up, tearing the fabric of his coat from the prickly seat below him. Neave and the girl didn't stir—their breaths were deep and regular. Jack stood, one hand on the back of his seat to support him against the rocking of the train. The wheels thundered below them. If Neave and the girl didn't wake in all this noise, they wouldn't wake if Jack stole away.

He stepped out of their dark alcove and into the main

space of the car. Two others were sitting near to the windows, one with a book in front of her face and the other staring outside at the expanse of green passing below the train. Jack lowered his eyes and held on to the luggage racks as he made his way across the car. Theirs was the last passenger car before the cargo cars near the caboose of the train; if he could get to the cargo cars unnoticed, he could return before Neave and the girl knew he was gone.

The space between carriages was cramped and shadowy. An Adrudian lantern mounted on the wall had run out of light, but Jack didn't bother to look under the slats to see if there was any glowing ore left. Instead, he rattled the handle of the first cargo car. It was locked with a hanging padlock. He examined the lock before crouching and pulling a long, silvery needle from his pocket. It was the same lock pick he'd used to break into a hidden puzzle door at Fort Upper's library just days ago. The books he'd stolen were tucked inside his jacket: *Gravel and Lode: Rocks and Gemstones of the Shute,* from a library shelf, and *Ancient Benemournian Rituals and Their Uses,* from behind the secret door.

After some jimmying, the padlock clunked and slid open. Jack pocketed the lock pick before unlatching the door to the cargo car and slipping inside. Dusty light fell around the edges of the car's removable roof. Jack hunched up his shoulders against the cool air, stepping over piles of crinkled packing paper and edging around stacks of wooden crates. He pulled open the door at the end of the car and moved on to the next.

The second cargo car was nearly empty. A lone metal tub sat in the very corner. Jack stared at it. He recognized its shape. He filled those tubs himself when the mill warden, Rhody Charlotte, gave him the job.

Jack hurried over to the tub, stumbling on the uneven, rocking floor of the car. The rumble and screech of the train's wheels was deafening. In the distance, the train's whistle sounded out. Jack's nerves bunched in on themselves.

He felt underneath the lip of the tub's lid, found the latch, and pushed. Orange light sprung from inside. Sighing, Jack reached in and sank his hand into the pile of Adrudian, stirring the rough rocks around. The ore was light and porous enough to have been candy. This was cooked but otherwise unprocessed Adrudian, shipped rough for use in engines, not smooth for lanterns or lights.

Or men, Jack thought, selecting a rock of ore about the size of his thumbnail.

Keeping one hand on the edge of the tub, Jack sat down against the wall of the car. Freezing metal pressed into his back, giving him goosebumps. His stomach fluttered.

She has a message for you.

He fished a match out of his pocket and set the rock of Adrudian on his tongue, tilting his head back. The ore was airy on his tongue, barely there. Holding his breath, Jack struck the match and brought it to the rock. It ignited. He closed his mouth and the fire went out, but Adrudian Milk was already sliding down his throat, piping hot. He swallowed the ore whole and let out his breath.

The door to the car slid open.

Jack jolted to his feet. He tipped backward on the seesawing floor and hit the metal wall, pain washing through his bruised shoulder.

A man stepped through the now-open door of the cargo car. The train rocked, but he stood firm without holding on to anything. Cold light trickled over his black coat from above.

"Well, well," Donborough said. He tugged on the fingers of his crisp white gloves, peeling one off, then the other. "*Someone's* predictable, don't you think?"

Jack pushed the back of his arms into the wall behind him, as if he could force through the metal like paper. "No ... not now." His mouth wouldn't obey him. His tongue was heavy, numb. "N-not—"

Donborough took a step closer. He sneered, lips parting to show a row of yellowing teeth. "Just you and me now, Blueveins." The gloves were stuffed in his back pocket. He rubbed his bare hands together. Jack tried to focus on them, but his vision was blurring in and out. "I like to laugh. Let's laugh together, you and I."

Jack's arms turned to iron, rigid and unmovable. His mind pulled away. The Watchman's face shifted in front of him, like an image rippling through a sheet of water.

The resting period was over.

"Goodnight, Drinker," Donborough said, and punched Jack so hard in the face his nose broke and erupted in warm blood. He fell backward ...

... BACKWARD ALL THE *way through the floor, as if he were the minute hand on a clock, all the way until he was inverted. A sea of blackness surged around him. His arms dangled above his head, reaching toward a yawning void, so vast he couldn't see where it ended or began.*

His fingers flexed, dreamlike and slow. He looked around—darkness in every direction. Still, he could see something forming, a patch emerging from the void. It was bigger than he was, bigger than even the train car had been. Jack's body drifted toward it, as if caught in syrup-thick gravity.

"You have heard my call," a female voice said. It seeped into Jack's brain as if the speaker were whispering into both his ears. He had never heard the language before—Ancient Benemournian? Maybe, but a dialect he had never come across. He seemed to be able to understand it anyway. Wiggling, he tried to take his notebook out of his pocket, but then he remembered Donborough had taken it.

"Where am I?" he whispered. The thing taking shape before him didn't answer. It was wider than it was tall, and jagged, somehow, like a shard of broken glass. Jack shivered. "What are you?"

"I'm someone like you," the wedge of darkness replied. "Someone who looks through doors. Someone who wants to be free. I've been calling to you since we met. You've felt it. I know you have."

Jack stopped struggling, letting his fingers dangle. She was talking about the pull, *wasn't she? The strange, painful longing that had planted itself in his heart since his failed expedition?*

The empty air was pushing on his chest, making it hard to breathe—but maybe here he didn't need *to breathe.*

"Let me free you from your anguish, Jack Fael. Let me show you my House of Matchsticks." The thing's outline was clarifying. It wasn't an object—it was a hole, a deep opening in the void. Jack was reminded of a crevice ripped into the ground after an earthquake. "Let me into your mind, and I'll show you your lost expedition."

The skin on Jack's back broke out in goosebumps. The lost expedition—the expedition he and Cameron had undertaken to find the House of Matchsticks a year ago. The same expedition that they had both lost, somehow, the memory burying itself in their brains.

Jack swallowed a dry lump in his throat. "How?"

"The lock. Look through the lock."

For an instant, Jack saw a red pendant floating in front of him, its center adorned with a cutout in the shape of a keyhole. He tried to grab for it, but it disappeared, dissolving in a puff of smoke.

"Then what?" Jack blinked, trying to bring the

approaching crevice into focus. It was coming straight for him—coming to swallow him up. Cold fear rippled through his body. "Drink Adrudian?"

The voice let out a grating laugh, loud enough to shake Jack's eardrums in his head.

"Foolish man," it said. "I am *Adrudian."*

Jack tried to yell, but his mouth was glued shut. The crevice approached, deep and dark. He was going to disappear down its throat, gone forever into whatever craggy place lay in wait.

A warm blast of sweet, rotting breath blew the hair back from his face. There was nothing he could do. It overcame him. He fell down

down

down.

He opened his eyes. Dusty light fell from the cracks in the cargo car's roof overhead. Sounds came to him slowly, as if from underwater. The rhythmic rumble of wheels. The squeak of metal against metal. Beneath him, the floor vibrated, sending lightning strikes of pain up through his skull.

Groaning, Jack sat up. His front was covered in blood from his broken nose. A tender bruise crept over his ribs, the mark of another punch or two, but his stolen library books were still with him.

He was alone. The *pull* thrummed in his chest.

2

THE HARPER AND CUP

ISALINE

After a long, winding descent down a seaside cliff, the train pulled into Lower Train Station with a seat-rocking rumble. Isaline stood in the train's tiny bathroom, rubbing cold water over her face, trying to shock life into her numbed skin. She had changed out of her filthy Survival Portion outfit, but her day clothes felt awkward, as if they didn't fit anymore.

Isaline put her hands on either side of the sink basin, hunching her shoulders and taking long breaths.

Calm down, she told herself. *Calm down, calm down, calm down.*

A sharp rap on the door made her jump. Jack's voice was muffled by the tarnished metal of the wall.

"Hurry up, Nalissa, everyone's off the train."

Isaline winced hearing her best friend's name. Nalissa was dead—she *knew* that—but last night wouldn't take root in her mind. Part of her was panicking about having to tell Nalissa what she'd done. How could Isaline ever explain why she took her train ticket into a new life? How could Isaline express that she couldn't leave Casret Academy on her own—that stepping into another identity was easier than facing the consequences of failing her Weeklong Review?

She pushed back from the sink, shaking her head. Nalissa would never have understood. Her path had always been carved out for her in the Quandary; she might never have made such a decision.

Isaline slid open the bathroom door and revealed Jack, leaning against the wall of the train with his arms crossed loosely over a wet patch at the front of his coat. He had washed his face and clothes, but it was obvious he had been in a fight. The bridge of his nose was purple, stringing a dark line between the veins twisting up the sides of his face. He and Isaline had the bruises in common—she'd scrubbed at her face, but her Weapons Portion injuries were barely a different shade from yesterday.

Neave stood next to Jack, fussing with the collar of her black coat. She had ignored Jack's new injuries, and didn't seem interested in how Isaline's bruises felt. Isaline was grateful, and suspected Jack was, too.

The door to the outside shone straight ahead, so bright it was almost blinding. Neave gave Isaline a friendly smile and gestured down the steps with the top of her head.

Isaline's scalp tightened. She had no idea what lay beyond that door—but whatever it was, Nalissa would have been ready to see it. The thought dampened Isaline's nerves. She clenched the sling of her stolen trident and walked down the steps.

Outside the train, Neave led Isaline and Jack over a large, wood-beamed platform and through Lower Train Station's expansive foyer. The three of them were tiny droplets trickling through a rolling wave of people swerving their luggage and brandishing their pocketbooks. A low wooden archway passed above them. Evening sun met Isaline's eyes on the other side. She blinked, realizing they were outdoors. She was standing atop a narrow wooden staircase leading down to a white beach. Sand reached to either side and circled a cluster of buildings to the north that must have been Lower Village.

Neave opened her coat against the warm, sticky air. She glanced at Isaline, her green eyes glinting. "You ever see the ocean before?"

Isaline couldn't find the words to respond. She gazed out at the tossing sea laid out before them, sparkling in the late sun. Its surface was speckled with bobbing boats and flickering Adrudian lamps, giving her the impression of a twilight sky flipped onto its back.

"You get used to it," Neave said, starting down the staircase after Jack, "eventually."

At the bottom of the stairs, Isaline bent and ran her hand over the surface of the warm sand on the beach.

Fine, gritty grains worked up between her fingers. She took a deep breath. The air smelled of burning Adrudian, but it mingled with a salty aroma that she'd never smelled before. She realized with a start what it was.

Nalissa, you were right, she thought. *The sea smells like salt.*

The memory reopened the burning hole in Isaline's chest. She forced the feeling down and held her breath, following Neave and Jack over the beach toward a long dock jutting over the water. She couldn't think about Nalissa. She could only keep walking.

They joined the end of a line of travelers on the dock, standing and waiting to board the ferry floating at the end. The ferry was small and ramshackle, made of discolored, warped metal. Its hull was splotched with black scorch marks, as if it had spent too long in an oven.

Neave tightened the buckle of her weapons belt. "The Captain's ferry has seen better days, looks like." She turned to Jack. "You seeing this?"

Jack made a sound that could have been a snort if his nose wasn't broken. "Always looked like a pile of scrap metal to me."

"It looked significantly better before you and Cameron set it on fire," Neave said.

"That was ... an accident," Jack replied, rubbing his fingers over his arm.

Isaline stared at him. He didn't seem the type to set a ferry on fire. He looked too tired, like he hadn't slept in months. The dark leather jacket he wore was shabby, his tie loosened to reveal pallid collarbones. One hand hovered at his waist, playing with the loops of his belt. Isaline guessed he was a Treasurehunter, too, even if he wasn't wearing a weapons belt or an orange Treasurehunter's pin.

"Don't worry, Nalissa," Neave said. She bent and tucked the legs of her trousers into the tops of her boots. "The ferry hasn't sunk in the years I've been taking it. Captain Knots is a capable seafarer, even if he *is* a scoundrel."

"And a fireworks smuggler," Jack added.

Fireworks. Isaline had never seen one in person, apart from the flare she'd set off in the training area, which had forfeited her Weeklong Review. She imagined the sparkling, lilac light of the flare multiplied by a thousand, shooting from the deck of a burning boat. The thought made her shoulders tense.

Neave glanced across the water, eyes roaming the horizon. Her eyes flicked to Jack. "Your friend from the train is looking at you."

Isaline followed her gaze toward another dock running parallel to theirs. At the head of a line of waiting travelers was a man with his face turned toward Jack. His grin was visible even from this distance.

"At least he's not taking the ferry." Neave adjusted her braid over her shoulder, lowering her voice. "I don't like Watchmen with smiles on their faces."

Jack said nothing. He had gone still as a tomb, his lips pressed together in a tight line. Isaline looked past the Watchman, searching the darkening water for another ferry. There were none—only tankers and sailboats.

"That Watchman," she said. "He's not waiting for a ferry over there?"

Neave's lips quirked. "A ferry of sorts." She pointed one black-tipped nail to the sky. "Look."

As if on cue, the sound of a beating engine filled the air, drowning out the sweep of waves on the shore. Isaline goggled as a massive, ballooned airship materialized out of the clouds, descending over the water near to the other dock. Thick ropes ran along the balloon from top to bottom, making it resemble an immense, peeled white orange.

The ship touched down into the water in front of the other dock, churning the sea. Passengers began to disembark the airship and make their way toward Lower Train Station, heaving their luggage.

"Where ... where does it go?" Isaline couldn't fathom what it would feel like to fly through the air in such a machine. "Where does it take them?"

"Ar, of course." Neave pointed over the rolling waves, to a distant mountain range lining the horizon.

Isaline's stomach somersaulted. "That's Ar?

"That's Ar, all right. Every brick and iron bar of it." One side of Neave's mouth lifted as she stared toward the mountains. "We won't get there as fast as that airship, of course. But we'll get there."

We'll get there.

Isaline wound her fingers into a knot, watching as a hatch opened in the airship. A woman in a blue pilot's uniform fed out a long nozzle attached to a hose. With a thick splash, a flood of Adrudian Milk rushed into the sea —byproduct from the ship's engine. The Milk dispersed into the water like a cloud of orangish ink.

Isaline was going to Ar, Benemourne's capital city. Not as a City Watch like she'd planned, but as an imposter. She swallowed. The burning in her chest remained numb as long as she kept moving. If she kept moving, she wouldn't have to step off her best friend's clear-carved path.

"Nalissa," Neave called. "Come on."

Isaline looked up and found the line had started to move; Jack and Neave had already made their way toward the ferry. She gazed at the airship for a split-second more before adjusting the trident over her shoulder and hurrying to join them.

Captain Knots turned out to be an enormous man in a shabby captain's coat. His gray beard was patchy, and his green eyes twinkled above a large, pock-marked nose. He didn't look at all trustworthy, but Neave was right: the ferry didn't sink on their way toward Ar. It creaked and groaned as if it might fall to pieces, but it held.

"Any trip could be her last!" Captain Knots yelled jovially over the pounding engine. He seemed to get some joy from the nervous faces of his passengers.

Isaline stood at a deserted edge of the deck, glancing at the approaching city and trying to remember to breathe. The water that rushed below them was open sea, swirling and fathoms deep. Neave appeared beside her, leaning on the railing.

"That's the mill." She nodded to a tiny cluster of lights sliding by in the distance. "The Adrudian mines are underneath."

A line of smoke emerged from the distant island and disappeared against the darkening sky. Words from Nalissa's letters teased Isaline's memory. *Mill. Mines. Listening Spider. House of Matchsticks.* She had disregarded them before, not knowing what they meant.

"The night's darker than it used to be." Neave tented her fingers, looking through them to the foaming water below. "Perhaps you've noticed ... the lights are going out. There's less and less Adrudian to go around."

Isaline bit her lip, watching the horizon. "The Adrudian mines ... are they emptying?"

"Maybe. Maybe not." Neave fixed Isaline with a smile. The tips of her canines were longer than the rest of her teeth. "Out there, at the mill, King Faraday's made it punishable by death to enter the mines. Only clockwork pickaxers are allowed underground."

Isaline envisioned the clockwork she had fought during her Weapons Portion, a giant with a head like a blank, wooden moon, lurching through dark tunnels deep under the earth. Cold fingers crept up her spine.

"There's something hidden down there," Neave said. She kept her voice hushed, but she sounded excited, like a cat that had come across an unguarded bird's nest full of eggs. "Something King Faraday doesn't want anyone to find: his workshop, where he designed his mysterious clockworks. I would bet gold it's connected to the missing Adrudian."

The little bunch of lights on the horizon twinkled. Isaline thought about her jewelry box, peeking out from behind Nalissa's hip. "How do you know?" She drummed the cold stone of the pendant through her shirt. "The King couldn't keep his workshop secret from *everyone*, could he?"

"He could," another voice said. "He does."

Isaline turned. Jack had appeared behind them, reclining on one of the ferry's empty metal benches. He had a book open in one hand.

"Faraday's made a habit of coming to the mill." Jack stretched his legs on the bench, crossing his ankles. "After hours. The warden told me before I left."

Neave leaned backward on the railing, folding her arms. "The warden just *told you*?"

"Well ..." Jack flipped a page in his book. "I bribed her with a bottle or two. That's not the point." His blue, hooded eyes were shadowed in the light from a string of lanterns reaching across the deck. "According to her, Faraday hasn't been to the mill in a long time, but all of a sudden, he's showing up in his red-sailed warship again, going down into the mines. He *is* keeping secrets. And paying Rhody Charlotte handsomely for it."

"Bribery." Neave tossed her head back, laughing.

"He's not above it," Jack said.

"I don't mean the King," Neave replied. "*You*. Cameron always wondered how you knew what you knew. You've been running Ar's distilleries dry."

Isaline looked down at the rolling water. Secrets. Bribes. Nalissa had never been a true Watchling if she'd run with people like this—but a twinge of uncertainty gnawed at her middle. She *had* noticed the nights getting darker. Even in Fort Upper, the roads had been barely lit. What if Adrudian *was* disappearing?

Isaline shivered, pulling her overcoat more closely around her. "So... why do you need me? A—a Thief?"

"Someone has to break into the mill, don't they? But it's your Watchling training we *really* need, ironically enough." Neave stood up from the railing, rolling her shoulders. "We'll go at night, when the building is closed. Empty—but there's clockwork guards to worry about inside." She saw Isaline's expression and winked. "You'll be fine. I saw your Weapons Portion."

Isaline wondered how Neave could possibly think that, considering the sparring clockwork had beaten her into dirt. She made a concerted effort to keep the memory from locking her knees.

Still, Neave's implication was clear: only a Watchling had any chance of destroying clockwork guards. Watchlings were the only people the King allowed to spar with his clockworks, and solely during standardized tests like the Weeklong Review. The odds weren't good, but more than nothing.

"Why is the King going down there?" Isaline asked. "Into the mines?"

"We don't know." Neave smiled at her, then strolled across the deck. Lanterns rocked on their lines, swaying with the beat of the ferry's engine. "But I smell treasure, Thief. And I have a good nose."

THE NIGHT ROLLED IN, and Ar rose up, a glittering colossus. Captain Knots docked the ferry at the edge of a wood-planked walkout. Ahead, past a strip of beach covered in fine sand, was the city: a towering slope of buildings so high and wide Isaline couldn't see where it ended or began. Looking at it, her vision blurred like water spotting fresh ink.

A throng of people disembarked the ferry, carrying Isaline, Neave, and Jack with them. Captain Knots stood by the ferry's exit, nodding at passengers and offering his hand to help them out of the boat. As Neave approached, his face burst into a broken-toothed grin.

"Captain," Neave said, offering her hand.

"Neave!" Captain Knots wrung her hand in an enthusiastic handshake. "And Jack Fael—what a treat—haven't seen you for months." He clapped Jack so hard on the back that he almost stumbled. "Where's your friend, the blond one?"

Jack muttered something inaudible, his lips pressed into a tight line. Isaline stepped off the boat behind him.

"Who's this?" The captain's cheeks turned into two round apples when he smiled. The smell of tobacco surrounded him like a cloud.

"Nalissa," Isaline said.

Knots gave her a bone-crushing handshake. "Any friend of Neave and Jack's is a friend of mine." He leaned closer, his bird's nest of whiskers gathering. "Neave buys most of the fireworks I bring in. You need any fireworks?"

Neave put a hand on Isaline's shoulder and pressed her on after Jack. "Knots. Does she look like she needs any fireworks?"

The captain stuck his hands in the pockets of his blue coat. "Never know," he said, and winked. "Safe travels."

Jack led them across the walkout. Isaline held her breath as she took her first step onto Ar's soft-sand beach. The sun had disappeared below the horizon, and the air was tinted blue with twilight. Adrudian lanterns glowed on wooden poles along the beach, illuminating ratty-cloaked merchants behind makeshift stands. Travelers and city folk milled about, faces doused in shadows, footprints mapping their paths.

Isaline lifted her eyes and gaped at Ar's soaring Watch Wall, a line of seashell-white stone arches surrounding the base of the city like a row of giants holding hands. Her skin rose with goosebumps—it was taller than anything she'd ever seen. Hundreds of City Watch perched on the edges of the Wall, pepper-sized, legs waving over the drop. Beneath them, the archways were supported by enormous columns. Iron staircases wrapped up the columns like strips of black ribbon. Isaline gazed at groups of Watch hurrying up and down the stairs, torches held in hand like minute, flickering stars.

Neave cut across the beach and led them toward a row of buildings tucked against the bottom of one of the Watch Wall's columns, outside the city's borders. Windows glowed yellow in the sweeping dusk, cracked open and releasing the aroma of something cooking. Stands on the beach sold roasted meat and vegetables, but this smelled different, like bread and herbs.

As they approached the buildings, Neave stopped and turned, halting their procession. She looked at Isaline, painted lips in a small smile.

"Jack will take you from here." She flicked her head toward the low buildings. "Cameron asked me to pick someone up in the city, and I'm already late."

The warm, yellow light from the windows traced Jack's mess of black hair. He grunted. Neave gave him a pointed look.

"Get Minna to make her some food," she said.

At the mention of food, Isaline's belly rumbled. The meager supper she'd eaten the night before seemed years ago. Neave nodded at her and walked under the nearest archway into the city, disappearing among a crowd of people hurrying up from the beach. Isaline watched them funnel into the city in an undulating mass. The edges of Ar were so close—she could run inside in a matter of seconds—but a cold fear rooted her to the spot.

"Well, come on," Jack said.

Isaline dragged her gaze away from the city and followed Jack toward the low buildings. She wasn't ready to step off Nalissa's path yet, but when she was, the city would be waiting. She sank her feet into the sandy footprints Jack left in his wake.

They came to a stop in front of a hanging sign reading *The Harper and Cup.* A leaping hare curled around the lettering, its paws clinging to a gold chalice. A smaller sign swinging beneath declared *No Vacancy.* Isaline trailed Jack up the walk, pulling the trident's sling from her back. The end of the staff knocked against the nape of her neck.

Jack heaved open a green-painted door, releasing a rush of warm light, the merry sound of people talking, and that delicious baking smell. Beyond the threshold was a spacious and comfortable tavern. A large, shiny wooden bar lined one end, its collection of glass bottles and tankards gleaming in the light from a crackling brick fireplace on the wall opposite. Low tables and cushioned chairs were tucked up against each other on the hardwood floor, holding an array of people.

Jack led Isaline to a table wedged in between a group of long-skirted women and a couple eating from a bowl of stew. At the end of the bar, a group of three City Watch in their black uniforms huddled together, chuckling at a joke one of them had told. At another corner, a group of Shute Treasurehunters gathered around a map spread out on the tabletop before them. Orange pins identical to Neave's sat at their lapels, twinkling in the firelight.

None of the tavern's patrons looked up as Isaline pulled out a cushioned chair and sat at the empty table. Relief trickled down her spine. The tavern was crowded enough that she could disappear.

Jack stood next to the table, his hand resting on the back of his chair. His eyes scanned the room, peering out above the splotchy, purple bruise crossing his cheeks. He seemed to come to a decision, and rapped his knuckles on the tabletop.

"Stay."

Isaline's eyebrows shot up. "Excuse me?"

He regarded her intensely, then sighed and shook his head. "Best not to draw attention to yourself." He tapped his fingers on the table, softer this time. "So, stay."

Isaline made a face as he walked toward the bar. He

kept speaking to her as if she were a child, but she was sixteen. It wasn't her fault he had the attitude of an old man—something Neave and Captain Knots seemed to like about him. The woman behind the bar was smiling at him, too, a smile that lit up her entire face.

Jack sat gingerly on a barstool and gestured with the top of his head at Isaline. The woman looked in her direction and inclined her head, then signaled to a man pouring a drink at the other end of the bar. He hurried through a pair of double doors and returned a moment later with a large bowl, a spoon, and a piece of crusty bread thick with seeds and herbs. He brought them over to Isaline's table.

"On the house, Miss," he said.

It was a thick, fragrant stew. Isaline stirred it with the spoon and big cuts of carrots and potatoes surfaced. Her mouth watered.

Jack and the woman at the bar talked while Isaline ate. It was the best meal she'd ever had. Half the stew was gone before she even started on the bread. The weight of her empty stomach on her limbs lessened, bringing warmth into her hands and toes.

As she was dipping the last bit of bread into the stew, there was a loud yell from the bar.

Isaline looked up. Across the tavern, the three Watch that had been huddled together broke apart, laughter halting. A Watchman with his back to Isaline rifled through his overcoat. As he buried his fingers into his pockets, she glimpsed ivory gloves. Her breath caught. She glanced over to Jack, who had stopped cold as if paralyzed, one hand reaching toward his own bowl of stew.

"Which one of you shit-for-brains took my flask?" The Watchman's words were slurred by alcohol.

The other two Watch, a man and a woman, shook their heads and lifted their palms.

"You drink cheap liquor, Donborough," one of them said.

"We wouldn't take it," said the other.

The Watchman, Donborough, turned out another empty pocket and swore. The tavern quieted, though no one had shifted in their chairs to look toward the Watch. The couple eating at the table next to Isaline stared silently into their bowl of stew, hands folded in their laps.

Donborough smacked the bar with his hand, hard, as if trying to push it over. "Get hanged, both of you." He swung to face the room. Two splotches of red spread over his cheeks, hallmarking the corners of his wide mouth. Isaline looked over at Jack, but his barstool was empty. He had fled, leaving his steaming bowl of stew untouched. She pressed her fingernails into her bread. Did he just leave her here alone?

"Any of you?" Donborough said, addressing the rest of the tavern. He made to push from the bar but had to catch it as he tipped off balance. "One of you is a thief, and had best come forward before I find you."

Silence. A man at a table near Isaline looked up, but his friend caught his eye and shook his head. Donborough's face darkened. The woman behind the bar put her hand gently beside his tankard.

"Donborough." Her voice was high-pitched, strained. "How about we call it a night?"

Donborough glared at her. "Some Thief stole my flask out of my pocket." He set his wrist down on the bar, pointing at her with a lazy hand. "This wouldn't happen if you ... if you didn't let them in, Minna."

Thief, with a capital T. Quandary Thief. Isaline's mouth dried as if it had been filled with sand. There were *Thieves* here, outlaws who rebelled against the King. She gulped as the woman called Minna frowned, looking at the other two Watch over Donborough's shoulder. They pursed their lips and stared at the ground, unwilling to get involved.

"I let in those that I see fit for good conversation." Minna's brown-gray hair fell in her face as she spoke. "If you don't like it, sir, you might consider calling it a night. I'm sure your flask will turn up."

Donborough snatched a glass stein off the bar and threw it to the ground. It shattered against the floor, spilling half-drunk beer and bits of glass. "Show yourself, Thief!" He scanned the room, drunken eyes roaming back and forth. "Too many Thieves and Blueveins have crossed my path today. I'm losing my sense of humor."

Blueveins. A puzzle piece slid into place in Isaline's mind. Jack's broken nose—it must have been Donborough who had beaten him up on the train. She cast around the tavern as a silent second went by, followed by another. No one was willing to speak up against Donborough.

Isaline squeezed her eyes shut as Donborough reached behind him, searching for another stein to smash. It was shameful for a Watchman to act this way, even off-duty. How had Donborough gotten stationed here, in Ar? He could never have graduated from Casret Academy, could he?

She waited for another crash of glass, but it never came. Instead, the silence was broken by the sound of a chair being pushed back.

"Over here."

The tavern turned their collective heads. Isaline opened one eye. Her gaze roamed the crowd of nervous faces until it locked onto someone who had stood up in the middle of the tavern, rising from a low table.

Someone in a deep green overcoat.

Jameson.

Isaline stiffened. The piece of bread she had been squeezing fell out of her hand and into her empty bowl. Jame had been sitting with his back to her—she hadn't recognized his hair without blades of grass tangled through. Small black sapphires glinted from the lobes of his ears.

"I'm the one you want," he said to Donborough.

Heat rose to Isaline's cheeks. She'd forgotten—Nalissa mentioned she and Jame were meeting the same people in the city. He and Isaline had run into each other during

Isaline's Weeklong Review. They'd survived together, and fought a monster, and she'd forfeited her exam to save him. Two minutes talking to Jame and Isaline's lies would be exposed. Her eyes darted around the tavern. She couldn't risk him seeing her, but it was too quiet to bolt for the door.

Donborough's eyes narrowed so severely it looked like they had closed. His face scrunched as he lifted a finger and pointed at Jame.

"So, there *is* a Thief." His voice was somehow both slurred and needle-sharp.

"Sure there is," Jame said. He took a step toward Donborough. His newly-polished boots clacked on the hardwood floor. "If you're going to be bad-mouthing Thieves, you might as well say it to my face." He flourished a sparkling hand. "As far as I can tell, I'm the only Thief here."

Donborough put his hand to his belt, only inches from the hilt of his long Watchman's dagger. "Why don't you and I take a trip to visit the King, Thief, and we'll see about that smirk on your face." His mouth split into a long grin. "You are against the law."

Jame rested a palm over his chest in mock surprise. "I am? Because I could have sworn I saw you wrestle that flask away from a merchant on the way here tonight."

Donborough's eyes widened. "You're scared of me, boy."

"You're mistaken." Jame shrugged, crinkling the fabric

of his overcoat. "I'm not scared of you *or* that great slab of brass you call King."

Isaline's breath rushed through her teeth. *Treason.* Jame could get killed for that, and Donborough knew it. He flashed a wild, drunk smile.

"What did you just say?" His hand inched closer to his dagger.

Isaline had the urge to recoil from the impending fight. Her blush was deepening, the risk of Jame getting hurt sending her mind spinning. She curled her fingers around the staff of the trident slung over the back of her chair. Jame looked at Donborough, his eyes steady, and rubbed his hands together. The whole tavern seemed to hold its breath.

Then, suddenly, a loud scraping sound—another chair sliding back. The crowd's many heads whirled toward the noise. Isaline had been so surprised to see Jame that she hadn't noticed the man he'd been sitting with. The man stood up now, straightening his red tie.

"That's enough," he said.

The man was so tall that Isaline wondered how he could have folded his legs under the low tavern table. His Watchman's coat was long and expensive-looking, parting at the middle to reveal a silky white top underneath. A fringe of gold-blond hair fell across his forehead.

Isaline's breath caught. He had a shining badge above his lapel.

The Head Inspector.

Donborough paled, the redness in his face draining. His hand shot away from the dagger as if it had burned him. The other two Watch stepped back, too, their eyes widening.

"Head Inspector," Donborough wheezed.

The Inspector put a hand on Jame's shoulder and strode past him, closing the space between their table and Donborough in less than five of his long strides.

"It's time for you to leave." The Inspector clasped his hands behind his back. "You can get another flask, I'm sure, and this time you might decide to pay for it."

Donborough wiped at the sweat on his upper lip. "Sir, I—"

The Inspector raised a gloved hand. "No need to explain. Go home and go to sleep."

The other two Watch shuffled toward the door, their heads ducked low. One hooked his arm through Donborough's, tugging at him. Donborough took a few off-balance steps and peered around the Head Inspector's shoulders to where Jame was standing.

"You're sitting with—with this?" Donborough pointed at Jame. A dark rage burned beneath the shock on his face. "You heard what he said about the King?"

The Inspector didn't turn. "You would do well not to accuse a complete stranger of stealing from you," he said simply.

Donborough looked at the Inspector like he had grown

an extra head. "He's Thieves' Quandary." His eyes flashed. "And you're just a coward with a badge."

The other Watch gasped. The Head Inspector didn't reply, just flicked his head toward the door.

For a moment it looked like Donborough wanted to keep arguing, but he finally relented, letting himself be pulled toward the exit. One of the Watch opened the door, and a wash of cool air popped the warm bubble of the tavern.

Before leaving, Donborough turned and shot Jame a look of ice. His stare was so heavy with threat that Isaline shuddered.

Then the door swung shut and the Watch were gone.

3

APART
THE COLLECTOR

The Collector examined the Harper and Cup's hanging sign. It was made of thick, carved wood, wide enough to support his starling companion, Caladrius, as she hopped back and forth across it, a spot of bright darkness in the air. Holding the brim of his hat, the Collector stood across from the inn's green door, off the path, invisible yet keeping to the shadows.

"Why are we here, Caladrius?" he asked, flattening his feet against the sand.

Caladrius didn't reply. Her cutout silhouette drank the golden light spilling out of the inn's windows. Making note of her silence, a heavy discomfort pressed on the Collector's chest. Not long ago, they had been at Casret Academy, collecting the soul of a dead student hidden beneath a gray coverlet.

That is my purpose, the Collector reminded himself. Before three days ago, he had never needed reminding. For as long as the Collector's memory reached, he and Caladrius had traveled Benemourne, collecting the souls of the dead in the Jar of Lights. The souls remained in the lantern, swirling orbs of light nestled in the Jar of Lights' blue glow, until they were ready to leave the earth for whatever lay in wait beyond the stars. The Collector found the simplicity of his purpose comforting; he wasn't privy to the secrets of the universe, only his small part of the turning wheel.

Caladrius had been both companion and leader. She sensed the dead, and the Collector followed where she led. But something had changed after Casret Academy. Caladrius had pulled him across the sea with a haste he'd never seen from her, as if a fire had been lit beneath her wings. Now she'd halted their journey for seemingly no reason other than to wait outside this inn. The Collector gave her a perplexed look.

"Tell me what you're thinking."

She fluttered off the sign and circled the inn's window. The Collector peered in, leaning his face close to the glass. People were gathered inside the tavern, clustered at tables between a shining bar and a roaring fireplace. His eyes roamed the crowd until he saw her. The girl from the boat —the boat the Collector had pushed sixteen years ago, impulsively saving her life.

Isaline, her friend had called her, before the monster

in the dormitory had attacked and she had taken a different name.

A coldness descended on the Collector. Isaline was sitting as if her feet were nailed to the ground, her hands curling and uncurling in her lap. Lines of light winked off the silver trident slung over the back of her chair. She must have been unremarkable to the tavern's patrons, but to the Collector, she stood out like the burst of a lavender-colored flare against the night sky.

He turned from the window and looked at Caladrius, who had resumed her hopping across the top of the sign.

"This can't be right," the Collector said, his voice small in his throat. "The smell of death is nowhere in this place."

Caladrius didn't respond, only shook her wings.

"Are we following her, Cal?" The idea made the Collector shudder. Thrice they had ended up in the same place as Isaline. The first time they had followed the flare, and the second time, in her dormitory room, there had been a soul to collect. But this—this was different. "How can we just wait here and do nothing?"

Cooing, Caladrius tipped her beak toward the inn's door. The Collector stared at her, confused, then swallowed an alarmed gasp.

"You can't be serious," he said. "Go inside? There's nothing in there for us."

Caladrius ruffled her feathers. Her gaze shifted to the Jar of Lights hanging from his hand. For a moment, her bird eyes seemed to reflect the bobbing souls of Lillian and Philip Just.

"Cal." The Collector gripped the Jar of Lights so tightly the wire creaked. "We can't help them. Lives aren't for us to change."

He wished he had taken his own advice, sixteen years ago.

Caladrius tweeted, but her response was cut short by the inn's door swinging open. Startled, the Collector shrank from the path and pulled the Jar of Lights up to his waist. Three people barreled out of the inn: two Watch holding a third up between them. The door shut behind them with a loud *bang*.

"Get off me." The middle Watchman pushed the arms of the others away, running his gloves down the sides of his coat. His drunken eyes glittered like diamonds.

"The Inspector won't like this, Donborough," one of the Watch said.

"The Inspector *doesn't* like this," the second corrected.

Donborough staggered over the sand, stopped, then squeezed his eyes shut. "I'm going to *kill* that Thief next time I see him," he mumbled. "Put my dagger right through his scoffing neck."

"You can't—" one of the others started, but Donborough kicked the sand with the sole of his boot, sending a spray of fine grains over both of them.

"*Don't* tell me what I can't do." His mouth twisted into a grimace. "You're as bad as him, that good-for-nothing excuse of an Inspector. Not a year with the badge and he—he thinks he can order me around." He spat in the sand, wiping the back of his glove over his mouth. "I'd love to see you all hanged."

The Watch recoiled, wincing. They looked at each other.

"We'll leave you to your thinking, then," one of them said, and the other nodded. They hastened across the beach, leaving Donborough behind.

"Cowards!" Donborough yelled after them. He kicked the sand again, this time sending grains flying at the Collector, who let them sail through his body. "Kiss-asses!"

The two Watch vanished up an iron staircase, headed for the top of the Watch Wall. Donborough grunted and patted the pocket of his jacket. He reached in and produced a ratty, leather-bound notebook, which he tapped with his fingertip, thinking. Then he returned it to his pocket and stumbled around the side of the Harper and Cup, disappearing into the darkness between the inn and its neighboring building.

The Collector waited, but Donborough didn't reappear. He stretched his fingers against the Jar of Lights. Its three souls hovered, pressing against the lantern's sides. Caladrius fluttered off the wooden sign and came to rest on his shoulder.

"These are human affairs," he said to her, turning his head. "They have *nothing to do* with us. Have you really led us where no souls need collecting? Where no one needs us?"

Caladrius clicked her beak. She pointed it toward the inn's window. The Collector, understanding, shook his head.

"That girl doesn't need our help, Cal," he said. His heartbeat was picking up; he'd never disagreed with her about anything. "We have a different purpose. If we follow the living around, we might as well be ..." Breathing. Alive. *Human.* He couldn't bring himself to say any of it. The more he spoke, the more his fear grew thorns that stuck into his ribcage.

Caladrius rubbed the top of her head along his jaw. The Collector leaned into the warmth of her feathers.

"I trust you," he said, but he couldn't help himself imagining the feel of a rough gray coverlet beneath his palm. The dead girl in Isaline's room at Casret Academy—even collecting her soul hadn't felt normal, as it should have been. He glanced down at the Jar of Lights. What if whatever had changed in Caladrius was happening to him, too? What if he was going to forget his purpose and could never return to the way things were?

"We shouldn't be here." He lowered his chin. Caladrius squeezed her talons into the fabric of his coat. "I made a bad mistake, all those years ago. This change is because of me."

The door to the inn creaked open a second time, revealing a head of brown, curly hair. Isaline slipped outside and pressed the door shut, pulling the strap of her bag over her head. The Collector drew further from the path. The skin on the back of his neck tingled, hair standing on end. Seeing her was uncanny. She was an ill-fitting piece in the puzzle of the earth. An extra piece.

Caladrius whistled, raising her wings. Isaline stopped and turned her head in their direction. She squinted into the shadows. The Collector's stomach dropped through his feet—but she couldn't *hear* them; that was impossible. Caladrius clenched his shoulder as Isaline stood awhile, listening, then continued past them down the walk.

"She couldn't have ..." the Collector said, tucking his chin to stare at Caladrius. Isaline's gaze had cut through him like a knife, but she hadn't *seen* them. A knot wrapped beneath his ribs. It had to be a coincidence.

Isaline came to a stop at the end of the path, looking at the sparkling expanse of beach and sea before her. The last ferry for the night had emptied before the Collector and Caladrius arrived. Merchants had packed and dragged their wooden stands into Ar. The beach was near-empty, the shadows of remaining Watch or wanderers roaming like lost spirits on the sand.

The Collector drifted onto the path, watching as Isaline took a quick look behind her at the golden light spilling out of the inn's window. Her eyes were wide and glossy. Panicked about something. She pressed her arms tight to her sides, made to step out on the sand, hesitated, then stepped out in earnest.

Caladrius hopped from the Collector's shoulder and soared through the air behind Isaline, tittering. The Collector froze, clutching the handle of the Jar of Lights.

"No," he said. His voice came out unusually high. "Come back."

Caladrius ignored him, her stars growing smaller as she trailed Isaline across the beach. The Collector fought with himself. It was clear now; they *were* following Isaline, for some reason he couldn't comprehend. What had the Justs *said* to Caladrius? What did Isaline have to do with them? And why had his interference sixteen years ago made a difference only now?

He relaxed his fists. Reasons didn't matter. If he let Caladrius lead him this way, things were only going to get stranger. But without Caladrius, he was useless; he wasn't able to seek out death like she could. No souls would be collected either way, and his instinct had only ever been to follow her.

He had no choice. He walked slowly after them.

Ar came into view as he stepped out from the inn's shadow. It rose and glittered above him, ringed by the smooth, cream-colored stone of its giant Watch Wall. Isaline walked stiffly across the beach, her head tilted back so far it looked like it might fall off her shoulders. She gazed at the iron stairways surrounding the Wall's columns, gaping at the Watch running up and down like tiny ink droplets. The Collector wondered what it would feel like to see Ar for the first time—if it would be exciting, or terrifying, or both at once.

Isaline came up to the base of one of the soaring archways leading into the city, then stopped short, grinding to a halt. Caladrius cooed as the Collector came closer, circling back and settling on the brim of his hat. He stroked her feathers as Isaline stared into the city.

"Why is she stopping?" he asked.

Caladrius whistled quietly, tapping her claws on his hat. The girl had begun muttering to herself.

"Come on," she said under her breath. "Just one step. One step and you're inside."

The Collector looked past her, down the dark street leading into Ar. Buildings rose on either side, blotting out light from windows above. A scrap of paper skittered across the cobblestones, disappearing down the twisted path.

"She wants to go into the city." The Collector stared as Isaline's chin tipped up, looking at the expanse of mountain above her, the ends of her hair swiping the trident on her back.

Caladrius chirped in agreement.

"But she's never been here before." A pang went through the Collector's chest. Ar was impossible to navigate without a map or guide. This girl would get lost in the alleys and never be heard from again.

Isaline rubbed her hands together. She lifted one foot up, then put it down in the same place.

"She's scared," the Collector said.

Caladrius tweeted, as if to say, *Of course she is.*

Footsteps approached from behind. The Collector looked over his shoulder. It was the boy in the green overcoat—Jame, Isaline had called him—walking across the dim beach. He approached quietly, hands stuck in his pockets, eyeing Isaline as she struggled to step across Ar's threshold. The Collector stepped to the side, lifting the Jar of Lights out of the way as a slow smile spread across Jame's face.

"Leaving so soon?" he said, folding his arms.

Isaline froze, one foot in the air. She whirled. "*No.* No. Just getting outside for a bit." Her eyes had widened even further, two dark marbles. The color at her ears and the tip of her nose deepened in a blush. "I—I didn't think you'd noticed me."

Jame drummed his fingers on his upper arm, rings sparkling in the lights from Ar above. "You're obviously not from around here, then. People notice people here." He lowered his voice. "Especially Thieves and Watchlings."

"I *did* notice you," she said. Her hand went to her collar, fiddling with the red pendant. The Collector peered at the ruby red stone, catching a glimpse of the keyhole cutout. "Even though you look ... different."

"Oh?"

She nodded, and kept nodding for a moment too long.

"You're less ..." Her hand gestured vaguely in his direction. "Grassy."

Jame chuckled, rubbing a hand over his mouth. The Collector gulped. A nagging sensation was growing in his middle. It was the urge to inhale, like he had felt in the forest, when he first saw Isaline. He shifted, trying to shake it. Breathing was unnecessary, and though it was possible for the Collector, it was far too human. Caladrius sensed his discomfort and dropped onto his shoulder, grazing her feathers against his neck.

"You must have left Casret in a hurry," Jame said, looking Isaline up and down. "I only beat you here by half a day." He took a step toward her, sinking his hands into his pockets again. "Why *are* you here, anyway, Watchling?"

Isaline opened her mouth, but no sound came out. She glanced over her shoulder as if trying to weigh her odds of escaping into the city. Jame smiled gently.

"It's just strange, seeing the same Watchling's face twice in one week." He dug into the sand with the toe of his boot. "If I didn't know better, I'd think you followed me here to arrest me. Turn me in."

Isaline's face went bloodless. "No, no I didn't ... I'm not ..." She pulled her bag closer, hugging it to her hips. "I don't want to do that. Turn you in, I mean."

Jame considered her. "Well, then. Maybe you came to apologize."

The uncertain expression disappeared from Isaline's face. She glared at him. "Apologize? I saved your life!"

"True, I can't deny that." Stretching his neck, Jame undid the button at the collar of his shirt. He pulled the collar open, revealing a long, red cut and a smatter of freckles along his throat. Isaline stepped closer, squinting at him. Jame gestured to his neck. "Looks bad, doesn't it?"

Isaline said, "I've seen worse. That scrape ..."

"Yeah, that was you." Jame grinned, buttoning his collar again. "Remind me to stay away from Watchlings wielding branches."

"Good luck finding one."

"A branch, or a Watchling?"

"A Watchling. I failed my Weeklong Review." Isaline examined her feet. The trident's sling slipped off her shoulder and she shrugged it back on again. "I'm not going to be a Watch."

For a moment it seemed she was going to tell him more, but then she shook her head. The Collector balled his hands. It was frustrating, watching humans interact—and the urge to breathe was getting stronger with each second. The urge had a voice, a whisper in his mind:

Take a breath.

He glued his mouth closed, clenching his teeth.

Jame gave Isaline a reassuring look, his mouth tugging up at the edges.

"Stay," he said. "Come back to the tavern. We can buy

each other a drink." He held out his hand. "I'm meeting some people later, but there's time."

Caladrius chirped, squeezing the Collector's shoulder. Isaline stared at Jame's hand as if it were holding a wasp's nest instead of a friendly invitation. She wrung her fingers.

"I should tell you ... there's ..." She took a deep breath, searching for the right words. The Collector tensed at the sound of her exhale. "The people you're meeting. I know ..." Her gaze lingered on his open hand. "You want to have a drink with me?"

"I owe you one, don't I?"

"I guess." Isaline chewed her lip, glancing over her shoulder at the deserted street.

A flash of doubt crossed Jame's face. "Unless you don't want to," he said. "Or you have somewhere else to be."

"No, I—" Isaline regarded him carefully, then sighed. "Okay."

He blinked. "Okay?"

"Okay, I'll stay. But then I'll have to go." Isaline took his hand, shook it awkwardly as if they were just meeting, and marched toward the inn. Her boots sank into the sand, forcing her to totter with her arms held out for balance.

Jame arched his eyebrows, but he looked pleased. "All right, then," he said, and hurried to catch up with her.

When they were gone, the Collector slumped his shoulders, clutching his chest. The feeling of breathlessness was painful, and so alien to him he could focus on nothing else. Caladrius stretched and shook her wings, her small bird noises blending with the wash of the sea.

"Isaline." The Collector dug his fingers into his coat. "Every time we're near her, I feel like I'm holding my breath. It's not right, Cal. What's wrong with me?"

Caladrius sidled up to his neck and pressed her head against his skin. Air passed in and out of her beak, little puffs against him. A shot of ice went down his spine.

"You feel it, too? And you mean for us to continue watching?" His voice shook. The urge to breathe was dissipating, but his nerves were uncoiling like a spool of yarn. "You want to go to this gathering ... whatever it is?"

She tweeted and bunched his coat in her claws, two firm knots against his shoulder. The Collector shivered. He couldn't fathom the idea of entering a tavern full of humans whose souls were safe in their chests. He couldn't think to stand next to them.

Caladrius didn't loosen her claws. The Collector swallowed the knot in his throat, staring at the sand. Grains stretched across the beach until sand became sea, and sea became horizon, and horizon became night sky. A cool breeze swept off the rolling water and blew fine sparkling sand through his shoes. The stars winked.

The sand breathes as the sea breathes, and the stars breathe.

Not me, though. The Collector glanced at his shoulder. *Not Caladrius.*

"We are *apart*, Cal," was all he could say. "Meant to be

apart from all of this. There are places even you can't lead me to."

Still, Caladrius nuzzled his neck, urging him on. Her breaths against him seemed to say, *Follow me, follow me, follow me.*

4

LITTLE SPACE

ISALINE

Jame slipped a sparkling hand into the pocket of his overcoat and produced two pieces of silver, shiny in the warm light from the Harper and Cup's fireplace. He dropped the silver onto the tabletop in front of Isaline as she arranged her overcoat over the back of her chair. The inn had quieted in the wake of Donborough's rant, patrons paying their tabs and trickling out of the tavern. Minna, the woman behind the bar, went about collecting empty tankards and bowls.

"What are you doing?" Isaline asked, fixing her gaze on the silver Jame had produced.

"Buying you an apple cider." Jame leaned back in his chair and folded his arms. "Don't take this the wrong way, but you look like you could use a hot drink."

Isaline's lips tightened into something like a smile. "There's no other way to take that," she said. She reached into her canvas bag. Before leaving Casret, she had impulsively pocketed the money Nalissa kept in her bureau. Using it on Jame gave Isaline a guilty twinge, but she didn't have any money of her own. She fished out two silver pieces and set them next to Jame's. "Here. For yours."

Jame scooped up the four coins and pushed out from the table, his eyes glinting. "Great. Guess we're even, now." He wove his way through the tavern toward the bar, jingling the coins in his open palm.

"Guess we're even," Isaline repeated, but as soon as Jame turned his back, she sank into her chair and buried her head in her hands.

She had never felt so torn down the middle. If she stayed at the Harper and Cup, it was only a matter of time before she was revealed as an imposter. But she didn't have anywhere else to go. Ar had loomed so great and hulking that it had paralyzed her. Taking that first step felt like a free fall into an open mouth waiting to bite down.

Then there was Jame. There was no point in pretending to be Nalissa with him. He would know she wasn't the smooth-tongued, clever Quandary spy from his letters. Worse, Nalissa's voice kept echoing in her head: *I don't like him the same way he likes me.* Jame had a crush on Nalissa. If he found out she had died because of Isaline, he'd never talk to her again. The thought made the burning pain in Isaline's chest smart. He was the only friend she had here—the only person who knew her before all this happened. She couldn't lose his friendship.

Isaline let go of a shaky breath. No time to make sense of her feelings now. Jack had reappeared in the tavern after Donborough and the Watch had left. He was standing at the end of the bar talking with the Head Inspector, looking annoyed and tapping the toe of his boot. When he spotted Isaline, he would come and speak to her as if she were Nalissa, and Jame would know she was lying. There was no choice but to try to tell Jame the truth and plead with him to keep her secret.

Jame returned to their table with two frothy mugs of apple cider. He set one down in front of Isaline, dropping into his seat. She looked at the bubbling liquid and found she couldn't stomach a sip.

"To surviving," Jame said, holding out his mug.

"Right," was all Isaline could manage. She tapped her mug against his and watched as he took a drink. Over his shoulder, the Head Inspector was gesturing to Jack's face, no doubt asking about his broken nose. Jack pursed his lips. His eyes wandered the tavern until they locked on hers. Isaline's stomach flipped.

"Jame." She squeezed her fingers on the mug's handle. "There's something I need to tell you."

Jame tipped his head to the side, setting his cider down on the tabletop. "Hm?"

"I ..." Isaline's throat tightened. His earnest expression made her heart pound. "I haven't been honest with you."

Jack was coming toward them, stepping between tables with the Head Inspector trailing behind. Isaline took a deep breath. "I'm—"

"Nalissa," the Head Inspector said.

Isaline's mouth clamped shut. *Too late.* She glanced up as the Head Inspector pressed a long hand to Jack's arm, coming to stand beside Isaline and Jame's table. Jack shrugged away from the Inspector's touch, turning in a full circle and leaning against the wall behind them, arms crossed.

"I'm glad you made it here, Nalissa." The Head Inspector was so tall Isaline had to crane to look up at him. "I'm Cameron Agustin. I hope Neave and Jack were able to break you out of Casret without too much fuss."

Cameron Agustin. This was the man Nalissa had been writing to in her letters. Isaline flicked her eyes toward Jame. He had gone rigid, as if someone had slapped him across the face. Her hand jerked and a splash of cider ran down her fingers.

"It—it was fine," she stammered, mopping at the spill with her other hand. "Except for the monster, I guess."

Cameron reached into his pocket and offered her a perfectly folded handkerchief. He looked at Jack. "Monster?"

"Looking for the pendant." Jack sniffed, grimacing around his broken nose. "Neave threw it out a window."

Cameron grinned, mouth parting the spread of stubble dusting his face. He had sharp, handsome features, sandy skin, and Isaline was surprised to see a flicker of mischief in his eyes. She couldn't begin to understand why Ar's highest ranking City Watchman would be writing to her roommate, Quandary spy or not.

Isaline handed back the handkerchief. She could feel Jame watching her every move. "The monster," she said. "It ... almost killed the both of us, actually."

"Good thing it didn't," Cameron said, flashing another smile. He nodded to Jack. "Let's discuss this somewhere more private, shall we? Follow me, everyone."

He bade the three of them in the direction of the bar. Isaline got to her feet, wincing as Jame stood up so fast he almost toppled his chair. She waited for him to say something, but he was stunned into silence. She walked ahead of him. There was no point in telling him now. He knew. It was as plain as the expression on his face.

Just keep pretending, she said to herself. *Wait until the last minute. Then escape.*

Isaline followed Cameron behind the bar and through the door to the kitchen, pressing her full mug of cider to her middle. She felt so small she could fold up and disappear.

THE HARPER and Cup's kitchen was barely big enough to fit its two cooks standing side-by-side. They nodded at Cameron as he led Isaline, Jame, and Jack through the kitchen's swinging doors and around a sharp corner at the rightmost side of a wooden cutting block.

The smell of bread and herbs hung in the air. Isaline held her breath, afraid to savor the smell of the food. She noted every exit they passed—means of easy escape out of the kitchen—and flexed her fingers close to the trident slung over her shoulder. Behind her, Jame's eyes burned into the back of her head like hot rocks pressed to her skull. She couldn't imagine he'd try to hurt her, not after everything they'd been through in the forest. But that didn't mean he would keep her secret.

Cameron led them to a small, half-hidden door in the wall of the kitchen, nestled behind tall baskets of hen's eggs and leafy, dirt-streaked vegetables. The entrance was so low Cameron had to stoop to hold the door open for Isaline. She clutched her mug of cider and stepped past him, down a single tall step and into the lantern-lit room beyond.

"Welcome," Cameron said, "to our Little Space."

Isaline's mouth opened, a silent gasp. *Little Space* was misleading; this room was big, much bigger than she thought could exist at the heart of the Harper and Cup. Dusky, forest-green wallpaper lined the walls, peeling in places but rich in color and depth. A polished mahogany wainscoting hugged the walls beneath the wallpaper, dark wood shining in the warm, orange-tinted light of glowing Adrudian lanterns. The scent of Adrudian ore was imperceptible beneath the aromas of spices, beer, and the ocean.

"I decorated it myself," Cameron said as Jame and Jack stepped in behind her. "My team has been meeting here for years."

A long table, smooth and solid as a bar of dark chocolate, stretched across the room. A variety of cushioned chairs sat tucked underneath, with carved wooden legs and backs of brass. Above the table, a row of windows looked out into the alley space between the Harper and Cup and the building next door. Isaline caught a glimpse of beach sand before Cameron pulled a line of thick, juniper-colored drapes across the windows, protecting the space from outside eyes.

"Make yourselves at home." Cameron pulled a chair out and offered it to Jack, who ignored him and sat at the other end of the table. "The others should be here soon."

Isaline ran her hand along the wainscoting's smooth surface, her stomach churning. Until now, she'd been able to envision Nalissa on this journey—what Nalissa could have been doing or feeling, if things were different. Here, it was impossible. Isaline couldn't imagine what it would feel like to walk into a space like this and *belong*.

Along the far wall, rows of shelves held potted plants, books, stacks of yellowing documents, and a collection of labeled stones and crystals. The stones caught and held Isaline's eye. She walked over, peering at them. They were stranger than any stones she'd seen before: shiny chunks of plum-purple amethyst; glittering, sky-colored azurite; clear crystals that emitted a soft glow. Her eyes widened at a row of large, glassy opals. Splashes of red and purple unfurled at their centers, as if someone had injected them with colored ink.

"Souvenirs from the Shute," Jack said. He leaned his elbows on his knees, looking at her over his shoulder.

"They're wonderful." Isaline studied an angular chunk of bismuth, a pyramid of metal shining in a peculiar spectrum of blue-purple-yellow. "But there's no artifacts here," she said, scanning the rest of the shelves. "I thought Treasurehunters hunted for artifacts, not stones."

"They do." Jack turned to face her properly, scratching a hand over his jawline. He ran his fingers over a pair of twinkling gold hoops in his earlobe. "Treasurehunters don't *keep* artifacts. They return them to whoever owned them in the first place."

Isaline traced the dusty spines of a collection of books, letting her fingers brush the gilded titles. "You mean the artifacts were stolen?"

"Yes. Hundreds of years ago. Thousands of years, some of them." Jack's gaze traveled across the room, to where Cameron and Jame were shuffling through a stack of documents at the other end of the table. Jame was nodding, pretending to look at what Cameron was showing him, but Isaline could feel him watching her out of the corner of his eye. Jack didn't seem to notice. "Treasurehunters look for items of value taken and hidden in the Shute," he said, "then give them back to their owners in exchange for gold."

"But who hid them in the Shute in the first place?"

"Ritual-makers, if you go back far enough. But these days, anyone who thinks the forest will protect their loot. Monsters are treasure-hoarders by nature. But so are bandits, pirates ..." He looked her up and down. "Even some greedy Watch."

"Watch," Isaline repeated. She set down her cider and pulled out a seat, leaving one chair of space between Jame on her left and Jack on her right. She dropped her bag on the floor and leaned the trident next to her, well within reach. "I'm not a Watch."

Jack made a snide noise in the back of his throat. "You're not a Thief, either. Half a decade surrounded by Watch, and I doubt you could steal a weed if it was growing under your feet."

Isaline's mouth went dry. "You don't know anything about me."

"Sure, I do." Jack's icy gaze studied her, wandering her face. The veins on his cheeks were dark spiderwebs reaching to his temples. "I know you have that keyhole pendant."

"So?" Isaline covered her collar with her fingers, pressing the pendant into her skin. Jack's eyes were so sharp they were making her squirm. She lowered her voice, hopefully out of Jame's earshot. "I'm not keeping secrets."

"I'd bet you are."

Isaline's belly turned into a beehive. Jack shrugged and

crossed his arms, leaning back in his chair. Was he bluffing? Trying to wind her up?

"You ever look through the pendant?" he asked.

Isaline pulled her eyebrows together, frowning. "Look *through* it? Why would—"

She was interrupted by the door's latch sliding open. Jack's gaze moved across the room, breaking their eye contact. Isaline let out a relieved breath, then turned in her seat, squinting as a head popped into the room.

"Haven't been *here* in a long time," the new arrival said.

The door swung open, and Neave swept into Little Space, a whirl of draping black fabric. She stopped, grinning, and held the door for another woman coming in behind her, who was shorter and hardly had to duck as she entered the room. Her face was hidden in the swathes of a berry-blue scarf, and her fingers held a long matchstick.

"Surprise," Neave said, flourishing. The second woman unwrapped the scarf and revealed herself to be Winn Just.

The energy in the room shifted suddenly, as if lightning had struck the table. Winn's scarf fell away to uncover a cloud of black hair and keen eyes flashing against dark brown skin. No one moved, but Isaline could tell they were in the presence of a ruler; Winn had only to give them a soft, angled smile and everyone sat up a little straighter.

She's not really *royalty, though,* Isaline reminded

herself. At Casret, Isaline had learned about the fugitive Winn Just, hiding from the King after the overthrow of the Seven Thrones. But Neave had said things had changed—that the King had finally killed the last remaining Justs, only to keep Winn alive to be his right-hand engineer.

Cameron beamed and returned the documents he had been holding to the table. He clapped his hands, making Isaline jump.

"Hardly a surprise," he said. "We've been expecting you."

"Hello, everyone." Winn's voice had a pleasant scratch to it, like an old gramophone. She stowed her scarf in her bag and hugged Cameron tightly, popping the match into her mouth like a toothpick.

Isaline could do nothing but sit frozen in her chair. She would have sooner believed that a mountain could fly than believe Ar's Head Inspector could embrace Winn Just. She glanced over at Jack. He was looking pointedly away from Winn and Cameron's hug, his mouth so tight it was barely visible.

Neave latched the door and dusted her hands. "Even if you're not surprised to see her, *I* was." She undid the gleaming silver buttons lining her coat, shooting Cameron a glare. "You couldn't tell me I was picking up the *Princess?*"

"Slipped my mind." Cameron winked, sweeping Neave's coat out of her arms. He hung it up on a peg by the door. "Sit, please, both of you. I'll introduce us."

"I would have changed, at least," Neave muttered. She pulled at the cuffs of her blouse, rolling her sleeves up to her elbows.

Winn waved a hand. "No need," she said. She deposited her blue scarf into the canvas bag around her shoulder. "I'm not a princess. Not really. It's just a nickname." Neave offered her a seat, but she shook her head. "I'll stand. For now."

Cameron tucked into the table across from Jack, who was studying the carpet between his boots. Eyeing Jack, Neave rattled the back of his chair with her hand on her way around the table.

"Look alive," she said, flashing him her pointed canine teeth. "The Princess is here." She settled into the seat next to Cameron, resting her hands behind her head. "That's Jack, by the way, Princess."

Winn stood at the head of the table and pressed her hands flush to the tabletop. She smiled at Jack with the side of her mouth. "It's nice to finally meet you. Cameron's told me much."

Now Jack raised his head. He glanced at Cameron, blinked, then nodded at Winn. "Nice to meet you, too."

Cameron gestured across the table to Jame. "And this is Jameson, the Thief I was telling you about. His reputation precedes him, I think. He's the best they have."

Isaline had been looking around at each of them, a numb feeling spreading through her limbs, but Cameron's words sent a jolt down her spine. *The best?* Jame was only just older than her—barely seventeen. She whipped her head to look at him. Nalissa had mentioned his reputation, but he couldn't be *the best*.

He was already looking at her, tucking a lock of hair behind his ear with a bejeweled index finger. Isaline quickly shut her mouth as he gave her a secret kind of smile before inclining his head to Winn.

"It's an honor," he said.

An abrupt flicker of warmth grew in Isaline's chest at his smile. She didn't know where it came from, but there was no time to make sense of it before Cameron had shifted his attention to her.

"And this is the Quandary's spy at Casret Academy." Cameron nodded, looking at Isaline in an encouraging way that only made her throat close up. "She's left her post for us. And brought us the pendant we've been looking for."

Isaline opened her mouth to respond, but her breath rushed out in a soundless wheeze. She couldn't lie, not here. She needed to tell the truth—even if she yearned to keep pretending—but *then* what would happen to her?

Jame was staring at her as expectantly as the rest of them. If he was going to reveal her, it would be during this pause that she was supposed to introduce herself. Isaline inched her fingers toward the trident leaning on the table by her knee. She couldn't give him the satisfaction.

"I ... um ..." Isaline closed her eyes and counted to three, praying the right words would come to her. She lifted her heels, ready to spring out of her chair and fight. "There's something—"

"Nalissa," Jame cut in. He looked around at the rest of them. "This is Nalissa. Years in a Watch Academy and she's forgotten how to introduce herself as a Thief."

The room gave a quiet laugh. Isaline's mind stuttered, halting halfway through preparing to charge through the windows in a crash of glass.

Did that really happen? Did Jame just lie for me?

He smiled at her, eyes glinting. The flicker of warmth in her chest grew into a flood of relief.

Safe. For now.

"Yes," she said. She loosened her tight grip on the edge of the table, finger by finger. "That's me."

Winn seemed satisfied. She reached into the bag hanging off her shoulder, rifling through a collection of what sounded like metal tools. "You're welcome here, Nalissa," she said. "Thank you for bringing what we were looking for, and for offering us the help that we need. That *I* need."

Isaline bit her tongue, unwilling to say anything else. She set down her heels. The staff of the trident winked beside her, but she returned her hand to her lap.

Winn produced an object from her bag, something that resembled a round, wooden box. Studs and discs of copper adorned the outside, shining light in every direction. "Now we're introduced," she said, "we better get started."

As she spun the box in her hands, pushing buttons and rotating knobs all over its surface, Isaline swallowed away the dryness in her mouth. She stole a look at Jame. He had taken on a strange softness, as if he were simultaneously hard to see and the clearest thing in the room.

Little Space. Taking a deep breath, Isaline settled into her chair. She would never belong here—not like Nalissa—but she could sit here a while. On the table, the foam had disappeared from the mug of cider Jame had bought her. It left behind a round coin of liquid, glimmering in the light like molten gold.

Isaline reached forward and took a long drink.

5

EYE IN THE LOCK

JACK

Winn twisted the final copper disc on the wooden box and opened her palm. A whirring sound like the drone of a tiny engine came out. The box clicked. Eight strips of wood emerged from its sides and bent in the middle like fingers. Jack was reminded of the clinging balls of steel he used to scrape out the cooking vat at the mill.

"Thank you all for meeting me." Winn arranged the box level on her hand. Her voice wavered, as if she were nervous addressing a room full of people. "I know gathering with me is a great risk."

"Speaking personally," the Thief boy said, shrugging, "it's not more dangerous than usual."

Neave laughed, a sharp sound that echoed in Jack's sore brain. She propped her elbows on the tabletop, flicking her braid over her shoulder. "He's right, Princess. These days, everything is a risk."

Winn placed the box on the table and rubbed her hands together. The skin on her palms was rough, calloused. Jack had seen as much when she had hugged Cameron. He couldn't get that hug out of his mind. Cameron had said he and Winn were friends, but how close *were* they? Jack wasn't a child—he knew Cameron had romanced his way through Ar more than once. But *Winn Just?* Even for Cameron, that was cutting above his place.

Jack glanced at Cameron across the table. His tie was loosened, and his shoulders relaxed. He'd taken off his Head Inspector's badge, leaving a blank space at his lapel. The difference it made in his appearance was marked. He looked younger, less like a Watchman and more like the Treasurehunter he used to be, before all this. Before the House of Matchsticks.

Jack looked away, scrubbing a hand over his blue-lined cheeks.

"So, this is it," Jame said. He peered at the strange gadget, one finger tapping the side of his face. "The Listening Spider."

Winn slid it across the table toward him. He caught it and turned it over, studying the outside.

"I installed this device into the King's heart. Ten days ago, about." Winn pressed her hands to the table again. "I designed it. Built it."

Jame passed the Listening Spider to the girl, Nalissa. Jack squinted as she turned it in her hands. The box looked heavy, with polished wood curving delicately around its multitude of copper discs. It was fine workmanship, but Jack kept the praise to himself.

"This was ... in the King's heart?" Nalissa murmured. She tried to pass the box to Jack, but he shook his head.

"Not exactly in his heart," Cameron said. He reached across the table and took the box, a lock of hair falling across his forehead. "The King doesn't have a heart. He has an engine."

Nalissa nodded as if she'd known that all along, but her eyes made it clear she was shocked. Jack guessed Casret Watch Academy's classes hadn't included the detail of Faraday's metal body. It was obvious the girl knew nothing, Thief or not.

Cameron passed the Listening Spider to Neave, who seemed unable to take her eyes off its gleaming copper. She traced a line across the wooden legs.

"A machine where a heart should be is ... just that, a machine," she said, looking up at Winn. "Exploitable."

"Yes." Winn brushed a thumb over her curved upper lip. "My friends Lillian and Philip Just knew. Faraday can't tend to his own machinery. He can build clockworks, yes—an entire army of them, yes. But self-operation is impossible." She paused, resting a hand on her stomach as if checking for the movement of her breath. "Faraday's kept me alive to do repairs on his clockwork engine."

"So ..." Jame shook his head in amazement. "He's made you a surgeon."

"Of sorts," Winn replied. "While we were in hiding, Lillian and Philip spent years trying to discover the secret to Faraday's technology. To figure out how to destroy it and defeat his clockwork army. To rebuild the Seven Thrones and restore peace to Benemourne." She took the Listening Spider from Neave and stood it on her palm. "Thanks to their sacrifice, I've gotten closer than they ever could. I've become the only engineer in Benemourne to see the King's inner workings."

A beat went by as everyone took this in. Jack shifted in his seat. He wasn't inclined to believe everything Winn Just said, but her story sounded true. Why else would Faraday let her live?

Across the table, Neave's face stretched into a smile.

"Are the rumors true, then?" she asked. "Does his technology run on blood? Molten gold? Magic?"

Winn raised an amused eyebrow. "It runs on Adrudian, like everything else."

Neave groaned, throwing her hands into the air. She dug into her pocket and slapped a gold piece on the table in front of Cameron.

"Told you," he said, sliding the gold into his coat pocket.

"No imagination," Neave muttered under her breath.

Winn laughed quietly, tracing a pattern on the table with her fingertip. "Yes, like his clockworks, Faraday's body uses Adrudian. But it's ... wrong. Inside, his engine looks new, like it was built weeks ago. But the human parts —the parts that should have been there in the first place—they're gone."

A silence descended, then Neave said, "Gone?"

"Gone," Winn repeated. "Rotted. His organs, muscles ... everything."

Nalissa's eyes were wide enough to see the whites around her dark irises. "What are you saying? That he's—"

"A machine," Winn finished for her. "Yes. No amount of Adrudian can bring a dead man back to life. But Adrudian is somehow *keeping* Faraday alive. Even after his body's death."

A shudder went through the room. Jack pressed his hands into the tops of his knees. If this were true, it would be supernatural; despite being lifelike, the clockworks at the mill were still automatons. The king was another question. Faraday had thoughts. Planned. Talked. How could he do these things, and be a clockwork himself?

Neave held out an open palm to Cameron. "It *is* magic. Give the gold back."

"I don't believe in magic," Winn said, giving Neave a small smile as Cameron dug into his pocket. "But I believe there are things we do not yet know." She looked around, her keen gaze lingering on each of them. "We've long known the King has access to some secret knowledge. He used it to build his clockworks. And now he uses it to keep himself living, too. What we *don't* know—how to stop him

—lies somewhere in his workshop, in the Adrudian mines. I'm going to find out what it is." She paused. "Tomorrow night."

A hush fell. Jack waited for someone to speak, but they were all blinking as if a ghost had passed through the room. He sighed, laced his fingers, and set them on the table.

"How can you be so certain?" His voice came out flat and hard. "You have a hunch, that's all."

"More than a hunch," Cameron said. He gave Winn a meaningful look. "Show them. Let them hear for themselves."

Winn nodded and pressed the top of the Listening Spider with her middle finger. A scratching noise came out, followed by a voice. It was soft enough to make Jack strain his ears.

"*How did ... where have you been?*"

The words were barely audible over the thrumming of an engine. Jack inclined his head, listening with growing interest. That drumbeat could belong to no one but the King.

A second voice answered him.

"*Waiting. In the mines.*"

This was the strange, hair-raising drawl of the creature at Casret Academy. Nalissa and Jame exchanged glances. Neave caught Jack's eye. The King *had* sent the man-snake to Casret Academy to retrieve the pendant. But how could he have created an alliance with a monster?

Faraday again: "*In my workshop ... and now you're here. Then it must be ... she's awake. I—I should have known. My clockworks have been mining less Adrudian. She's trying to get my attention, isn't she?*"

"*Yes. She is growing impatient. She's given you time enough to enjoy the gift of her power. You must find what you lost, and try again to open the door.*" The creature's voice was obscured by static, then returned in reply to the King. "*Send me. I will retrieve the lock. Then you must return it to the mines, and to the House of Matchsticks.*"

There it is, Jack thought, swallowing the rise of energy in his limbs. It was strange to hear *House of Matchsticks* uttered by another mouth—it had been his secret obsession for so long, and now he'd heard it twice in one day.

Faraday's voice rang out next. "*How will ... the lock?*"

"*It is with the girl. In a Watch Academy. She doesn't know ... the wearer forgets. Send me. I will find her and ...*"

"*Then go,*" Faraday replied. "*Bring the lock. I will travel to my workshop tonight.*"

The conversation descended under a swarm of static, followed by a click, and finally nothing. Silence swept into the room. They all looked at each other. Then, like a balloon overfilled to bursting, everyone began to speak at once.

"That voice," Jame said. "That was the monster that came out of the woods."

"The King sent it. That's clear." Cameron replied.

Neave looked at Winn. "Who's the *she* they were talking about?"

"Someone in the mines." Winn chewed her lip. "I don't know."

Jack stayed quiet as the others discussed, his head spinning. Cameron had been right—Winn's idea wasn't just a hunch. But how could the House of Matchsticks be in the mines? His mind flew back through his research, the countless hours he'd spent skimming his fingertips over the pages of ancient books. The documents had been certain the House of Matchsticks was in the Shute. Jack *never* misread documents—and if he'd been wrong, what had happened to him and Cameron during that expedition?

The voice from his vision on the train came back to him: *Look through the lock.*

He eased his eyes over to Nalissa. She had covered her collar with her hand, staring wanly at the rest of them. It was clear she was hiding something—something about how she'd obtained that pendant in the first place. Cameron had said it belonged to her roommate, but it didn't add up. She was protective of it. Jack would have wagered the pendant had been Nalissa's all along, and now the creature on Winn's recording had all but named her.

Nalissa has something to do with this.

He had to take the lock from her—but how?

"Jack," someone said.

He started, looking up at the rest of the table. They

were all looking at him, waiting for an answer to a question he hadn't heard. A nervous ripple passed through him. He cleared his throat.

"What was that?"

Neave brushed her hands, leaning over the table. "The Princess asked what you know about the House of Matchsticks," she said. "What you found."

Jack swallowed, then tipped his chin in Cameron's direction. "Might as well ask *him* the same question."

"Actually," Winn said, waving away Neave's reply, "I'm asking you." She fixed Jack with an interested stare. "Your research was ahead of Cameron's, wasn't it?"

Cameron made a startled noise. "Not *that* much ahead," he said quickly. "But sure."

Jack bit the inside of his lip. Their attention quickened his heartbeat—especially Cameron's, whose gaze always made him jumpy, like he knew something Jack didn't. But the thought of clamming up was worse than sharing his research. Jack ignored his racing heart, cleared his throat a second time, and started to speak.

"The House of Matchsticks is—is an ancient cave. I read about it in documents from Ar's archives," he said. "It's rumored to hide valuable knowledge. Could be a treasure, or an artifact, or both. No one knows the details, but the texts I found guessed it was hiding a keystone."

Jame tipped his head to the side. "Keystone?"

"Ancient-speak for a *ritual artifact*," Neave replied.

Her eyes gleamed. "Treasurehunter-speak for *you're going to get rich.*"

Jack nodded. "Keystones are objects that were used in Ancient Benemournian rituals. They're valuable to have."

"Why?" Nalissa asked. "Treasurehunters don't keep their artifacts. You said so yourself."

"True," Cameron jumped in. He crossed one leg over the other, casually revealing a fashionable, ash-gray sock peeking out beneath his hem. "But usually there's someone out there who wants that keystone back."

"And for a nice reward." Jame nodded, understanding. He looked over to Jack. "Does that mean there was a ritual at the House of Matchsticks?"

"It's probably a ritual site," Jack replied. He danced his fingers over his thigh, wishing he had his notebook to read from. "There's lots of sites in the Shute. Ancient Benemournians believed in various gods. They relied on rituals to bring them luck or prosperity."

"Or knowledge?" Winn asked, looking between Jack and Cameron.

Jack frowned at the suggestion. "If you're implying Faraday performed some sort of ritual for the knowledge to invent clockworks—"

"—it wouldn't be likely," Cameron finished. "The House of Matchsticks predates Faraday by thousands of years, and the gods probably never existed. Just stories."

Neave pursed her lips, tugging at the end of her braid. "There *was* a ritual there, though, with a keystone?

Who would go down into a musty old cave to perform a ritual?"

"I don't know," Jack said. "But the texts I found seemed to think someone did."

"Why is it called a house, then? Did somebody live there?"

"*House of Matchsticks* isn't a perfect translation. *House* simply means there's something inside the cave—it's housing something. *Matchsticks* implies darkness. Ancient Benemournians would have needed fire to see there, before Adrudian." Jack ran a finger around the inside of his collar, trying to loosen the tension that had captured his throat. The lost expedition wasn't a topic he was eager to broach, not with so many strangers. "The map I drew led underground."

Nalissa hadn't picked up on his tone. "You had a map? But you still didn't find the House of Matchsticks?"

"Not exactly," Cameron said flatly. He picked a piece of lint off his sleeve, fixing his eyes on the table. Jack guessed Cameron wanted to talk about their expedition about as much as he did. "Jack, did you bring the map?"

Jack exhaled, relieved to shift their attention. He reached into his pocket and pulled out a square of folded parchment. It was blind luck that he hadn't tucked it inside his notebook, which was still lost to that white-gloved Watchman. Jack opened the parchment and smoothed it flat, pushing it into the center of the table.

"This is the Shute," he said, gesturing to the entirety of

the map. "Up here is the entrance." He pointed to the northwest, where he'd drawn a pen-and-ink illustration of a large, gnarled tree. "The Dead Tree. And *this* is the path that should have led me to the House of Matchsticks." Slowly, Jack traced his finger down from the Dead Tree, along a line he had drawn.

"What's this?" Jame asked, pointing at a spiral at the west of the map. Jack's ink line passed through it.

"A plateau of some sort." Jack circled it with his fingertip. "The spiral is likely a rock formation."

"Likely?" Winn's mouth turned down. "You didn't get that far?'

Jack glanced at Cameron, who looked paler than he had a moment ago. Did Winn not know about their expedition? Across the table, Neave tucked her chin, looking just as confused. So, Cameron had kept their expedition a secret, even from close friends. Jack wasn't sure why, but the knowledge pleased him—so much he didn't know what to say next.

"We might have gotten to the plateau," Cameron said when Jack didn't fill the silence. He stood stiffly from his chair, bending to study the map. His head came so close that Jack could smell beeswax, the candle scent Cameron always seemed to exude. "The whole affair is a bit ... blurry."

"Blurry?" Nalissa repeated. "You can't remember what happened?"

Jack and Cameron exchanged looks. There wasn't an easier way to say it.

"Some kind of sickness," Jack muttered.

"Or enchantment," Cameron added.

Winn scrutinized them through a twist of her hair. "Enchantments don't exist." She pressed her hands into the table on either side of the map. "Why didn't you tell me this before?"

Cameron cleared his throat. "Not much to tell."

Jack rapped the table with his knuckle. "What we *can* tell you is where we ran into each other." He slid his index finger a short way from the Dead Tree. "And where we started forgetting." He tapped a spot close to the spiral plateau.

After the plateau, they should have come to a bridge, then traveled through a pin-straight passage southward until they found the House of Matchsticks. Jack had come to think of the passage as the *straight shot*. The inky black *X* he had drawn was at the bottom of the map.

"No memory ..." Winn sighed and pushed from the table, scratching the back of her head with one hand. "I was hoping this would be more useful."

"It *is* useful," Jack said. "The texts I read were clear."

"Texts can be wrong."

"Not when they all agree. Everything written about the House of Matchsticks mentions the Shute. My research was sound. It still is."

Cameron sat back into his seat, shaking his head. "Winn's right. What you tried didn't work."

"What *I* tried?" Heat flared in Jack's chest. He shoved the map across the table, crossing his arms. "Last time I checked, you were there, too, *Head Inspector*."

"Wait," Nalissa said, cutting off Cameron's retort.

They all turned to look at her. She was holding her hand out in front of her face. The keyhole pendant swung from her fingers, glimmering crimson in the Adrudian light.

"Could this have something to do with the Shute?" Her brown eyes followed the pendant as it swayed on its chain. "Jame said it might have been made of some kind of gemstone from the forest."

"Purpesia." Jame gestured to the pendant as Nalissa pulled the chain from around her neck. She dropped it onto the table. "My parents used to see it in their jewelry once in a while."

Neave lowered her head as if to look at the pendant at eye level. "Purpesia is said to be cursed. It brings bad luck to whoever takes it out of the forest."

"Fitting, in other words." Winn slid the map back toward Jack. "Here."

Jack folded the map, pushing it into his pocket and throwing Cameron a cold glare. Why did Cameron bother inviting him here, if he wasn't going to be *useful?* To make fun of him? Embarrass him?

Winn stuck a hand in her bag and produced some

kind of metal apparatus. It was bigger than the Listening Spider and strangely shaped, with a square base that had a sheet of glass stretching over its top like a window, and a brass arm reaching over the base.

"Glad I thought to bring this," Winn said, setting the apparatus on the table. She turned to one of the Adrudian lanterns hanging above the wainscotting and opened its slats, brightening the room. The sudden burst of light sent a bolt of pain through Jack's aching head. "Let's look closer."

Winn shook the lantern and a shining, smooth rock of Adrudian rattled out. She closed the slats and dropped the Adrudian into a compartment in her apparatus. A square of light appeared on the wall, running like water over Winn, lighting her waist and arms.

"A projector." Neave whistled. "I've never seen one before."

"I built this one. Years ago." Winn pushed the projector toward Jack, widening the square of light so it pulled over her head. "Now, let's see that pendant. Put it on the glass."

Nalissa hesitated, then held the necklace by the chain and stood halfway up, sliding the pendant onto the glass of the projector. As she did, it came into focus in the square of light on the wall. Winn was bathed in red, her blue skirts taking on a ruddy, plum hue.

"Good," Winn said. "What do we see?"

She moved out of the light, folding her arms. The

projection covered most of the wall, the magnified keyhole cutout big enough to resemble a broad doorway. A tingle erupted on Jack's scalp.

"Looks like purpesia to me," Neave said, pressing her fingers to her chin. "Not quite opaque. Glittery."

Jack squinted at the red gemstone. Something about the image seemed wrong; the pendant was distorted, too big and too small at the same time. He was having trouble keeping it in focus.

"It would take a powerful machine to cut a shape through a rock of Purpesia." Winn moved back in front of the projector and traced the outline of the keyhole cutout with her hand. Dazzling flakes of light seemed to swim around her fingers, making Jack's headache thump.

No, they aren't swimming, he corrected himself. The pendant was glittering, but the image couldn't be *swimming*. A trick of the light.

"If this pendant is old, it would be near-impossible to engineer a cutout like this," Winn continued. Light slipped over her features like liquid—and for a moment Jack had the bizarre impression that it *was* liquid, that Winn could press herself into the keyhole cutout and disappear. "And the keyhole shape is too clean to be natural."

As Winn swept her hand along the image, a high-pitched hum rose in Jack's ears. The fine hairs on the back of his neck spiked. Gulping, he pushed up the sleeves of his coat. His skin was tightening in gooseflesh.

Something isn't right, he thought. No one around the table seemed to notice. He looked back at the projection. It *was* swimming, rippling like the surface of a lake.

Winn glanced at him, eyes narrowing. "Jack? Are you—"

The light in the room changed.

IT HAPPENED WITH A LITTLE *POP*, as if midnight had been standing outside the door, waiting to rush inside. The lanterns on the walls dimmed, their Adrudian glow suddenly sucked dry. Jack recoiled as the red gemstone in the projection was swallowed—not disappearing, but shifting, the red transforming into a writhing, shimmering black.

Nalissa jumped, hitting her knee on the table. Her empty mug of cider clattered over on its side. "That's it." She drew into the back of her chair, staring open-mouthed at the wall. "It did this in the forest, when I looked at it up close."

Jack tried to speak, but his tongue was numb, too big for his mouth. His vision hazed. If he hadn't known better, he would have thought he was sinking into an Adrudian spell. But he hadn't Drunk, not since the train.

An indistinct shape at the head of the table—Winn, still standing in the center of the keyhole—craned upwards, gazing at the new, shimmering darkness. A slow stir of motion teased the keyhole's bottom edge. Jack squeezed his eyes shut, then opened them again. A darkness was spreading across Winn's skirts, a semicircle of inky light creeping.

The beginnings of a round, glistening orb was rising from the bottom of the projected keyhole like a black sun.

All the flesh on Jack's body crawled over his bones. Something was coming.

"It's ..." The shadow of Jame stood up out of his seat. His voice wavered in Jack's droning ears like a vibrating string pulled taut. "Is that—"

"An eye," said Cameron, and Jack's vision clarified all at once, bringing the projection into focus. The pupil was wet and glistening—a round, black coin. Winn stood in its center, surprised into motionlessness. The eye blinked, slowly, the image of its milky white lids dragging down and up Winn's body.

Across the table, Neave stood up like lightning. Her chair rocked into the wall and fell over.

"Princess." She stretched her arm out to Winn. "Move, now. Please."

Winn stepped out of the light as the rest of them got to their feet. Nalissa wrapped her fingers around her trident, bending her knees. Jame reeled backward less gracefully. He hooked his ankle on the leg of his chair, stumbled, then left the chair sitting at a diagonal slant in the middle of the floor.

Unlike the others, Jack couldn't stand. His legs

wouldn't obey him. The buzzing in his ears had risen to an ear-splitting pitch, so loud it glued him into his seat.

"Someone grab the pendant." Neave's hand flew to her side, but she had taken off her weapons belt. "Take it off the projector."

Jame lunged for the table, but the eye blinked again, startling him in place. Watery slime spread over its pupils and whites. Jack *felt* it seeing him. His mind squeezed in on itself.

Then the eye rose straight up, out of the keyhole, and was replaced by something Jack could only guess was a mouth.

His stomach lurched as it came into focus. Ridged, graying skin. Sliming and maggot-colored, huge on the wall. The mouth opened and the air in the room suddenly thrashed. Chairs slid out from under the table and crashed into the walls. The juniper curtains swung wildly, lifting over Cameron's head and wrenching at their rings. A smell like putrefying wood surged through the room.

"Take it off *now*," Neave roared over the din. Her braid whipped around in the wind, narrowly missing Cameron's face, slack-jawed behind her.

"Listen!" Winn backed into the wall, bracing against the pitching air. "It's saying something."

"*Help me* ..." the air whispered. "*I'm in a cage. Underground ... help ...*"

The rest of them gasped as Jack's vision darkened. A gust of wind hit his back, powerful enough to push him up onto his dead legs. The keyhole seemed to expand. His mind slipped through the floor like melting snow. He fell down

down

down ...

... DOWN INTO A DARK, *empty space, smaller than last time.*

He fell onto his knees, sending a fire-hot pain shooting up his thighs. The ground was pebbly, cutting through the fabric of his pants. At least he wasn't floating mid-air, this time.

The darkness was complete. He got to his feet, groped around, and came up against stone walls not three feet on either side of him. The stench of acrid smoke filled his mouth, stronger than it had been in Little Space.

"So, you looked through the lock," a familiar voice said.

Jack whirled, hand flying to his side for his dagger. There was nothing but blackness behind him.

"Look down," the voice said.

Jack lowered his eyes to his boots. The ground was swallowed in the dark.

A grating, high-pitched giggle echoed in his mind. "Down is up, *here, Jack."*

Dryness crept into his mouth. The voice was female-sounding, but had a second layer that was quiet and toneless, as if multiple people were speaking at once.

Holding his breath, Jack slowly lifted his head.

There was something kneeling on the ceiling. The dark swallowed its features, but he could just make out its shape; it was tucked up in the corner, pressing its face against the wall. A halo of white light shone around its head, too faint to push back the shadows.

Fear, sharp as a knife's point, coursed through Jack. Giggling again, the thing on the ceiling pulled its face from the wall. The light shining around its head shrunk to a tight, bright line emerging from the stone, through a small hole in the shape of a lock.

The eye looking through the keyhole.

"Yes," the thing said, as if hearing his thoughts. It got to its feet, standing on the ceiling. Jack shuddered. The top of its head hovered a few feet above his. "You're shorter than I remember."

Jack didn't know how to respond to that. He backed away until he bumped into the stone wall, heart pounding. The thing strode toward him. An orange gossamer dress draped its body, fabric winking in the faint light from the lock.

"Who are you?" Jack whispered.

The thing came to a stop just ahead of him, craned its neck downward—or upward—and faced him. Its face could have had a woman's features, if it weren't for the waxy, drooping skin. And her eyes—they were perfectly circular, black as obsidian, and unblinking.

"I've told you before, haven't I? I'm someone like you."

Her body lowered until her chin was level with the top of Jack's head. Jack glanced upward, expecting to see her feet floating in the air, but the bottom of her dress was still brushing the ceiling. She hadn't floated downwards—she had elongated, *lengthening her body to meet his height.*

"I don't mean to be rude," Jack said, "but you don't seem *to be someone like me."*

*She stared at him, her eyes two dark holes. A length of hair, matted and grease-black—*like mine, *Jack thought—fell down her shoulders.*

"Do something for me, Jack Fael." Her mouth stretched as she spoke, revealing a toothless, deep cavern. "Bring the girl with you."

Jack let out a short breath. "What girl?"

"The girl with the pendant. Bring her with you." She smiled, but upside-down it looked like a long, distorted frown. "We're trapped, she and I, and I want us to be free. Bring her, and if you Drink, I'll show you."

The expedition.

"Yes," she said again, and Jack was sure she could read his mind. "Keep this a secret, won't you? And let me in." She lowered her hands to his face. Jack flinched, but he was too afraid to draw his dagger. "Let me in."

Her fingertips touched his temples. A crack appeared in Jack's vision, a fracture that slid from one eye to the next. He yelled. The woman in front of him vanished, and the crack widened, letting in a rush of images that assailed him with the speed of a steam train.

He saw dark places, long tubes leading down through space, ringed with rows of sliming, waving black vines ...

He saw a crevice in the ground out of which a mouth grinned, a beetle turning in circles on one of its hooked, graying teeth ...

He saw himself falling through a crevice, down, down into the endless pupil of a massive, open eye ...

He saw Cameron, raised off the ground with his arms hanging, a tearing sound, a gurgle, a streak of blood ...

He saw ...

"JACK." Cameron's voice sounded as if it were coming from far away. "*Jack.*"

He opened his eyes. Little Space was around him. The Adrudian lanterns on the walls effused a weak glow, draping the room in shadows. The sudden wind had settled, leaving them in a heavy silence. Jack's hair hung in his face.

Jame groaned. He had dropped to the carpet on his hands and knees, taking in great gasps of air. Beside him, Nalissa was nearly horizontal, holding onto her chair so tightly it seemed her fingers would squeeze through the brass.

Jack saw all this from above, and blinked—he was standing on the table.

When did I get on the table?

He pushed his hair out of his eyes. There, out in front

of his face, was his own hand, holding the keyhole pendant. The bronze chain dangled from his fist, sparkling despite the weak light. Winn's projector lay at his feet, turned over on its side with its glass window spiderwebbed with cracks.

Neave's forearms appeared over the edge of the table. She smacked her palms against the tabletop as she hauled herself up from the floor.

"No ... *way* ... that's only a pendant." Her head appeared and she pressed her cheek to the smooth wood. "That voice ... I thought my ears would explode."

Jack ran the back of his sleeve over his forehead, wiping away streaks of sweaty hair. The pendant wobbled crimson on the end of its chain. How many seconds had passed since he'd fallen into the vision? Long enough for him to climb up and take the pendant from the projector.

Cameron heaved a chair up from the floor and slumped into it, rubbing his eyes with his fingertips. Behind him, the row of windows rattled, letting in a cool sea breeze. The latches had blown open in the chaos.

"Take all my gold," Cameron said. His tie had come askew, flopping over the edge of his coat. "I know you don't believe in it, Winn, but it's magic. Or something like it. The King—"

Jack made a shushing sound, forcing air through his teeth. He climbed from the table and pushed Cameron aside. "The windows blew open." He wrenched the panes closed and cranked the latches, locking them. "Do you want all of Ar to hear you?"

Cameron didn't seem to have the energy to argue. He just shook his head and rubbed circles into his temples.

At the head of the table, Neave turned the projector upright, examining the cracks in its glass. Its brass arm swung in a wild arc around the base.

"Broken." She pushed it away from her, letting out a long breath. "Sorry, Princess."

"I've never heard a voice like that." Jame bent down and handed Nalissa her fallen trident. He grinned as she flexed her fingers on the metal. "It sounded like two people talking at the same time. Weird, right?"

Jack opened his fingers and dropped the pendant on the table. It had barely landed before Nalissa scooped it up and threw it around her neck. He watched her for a moment, examining her panicked expression as she pressed her hand to her collar.

We're trapped, she and I, and I want us to be free.

How did Nalissa end up with the pendant—and what did the woman in the mines want with her? It was clear to Jack that the woman he'd spoken with was the *she* Faraday talked about on the recording, but how did it connect to this Thief girl?

A match flared, breaking him out of his thoughts. The pinprick of light revealed Winn Just, lifting the wooden end of the match to her mouth.

"That pendant," she said, her breath extinguishing the match in a curl of smoke. "It's the keystone."

They all looked at each other. The smoke from Winn's match spiraled up and around her head, running over her face like night mist.

"I have a hunch." Her eyes rested on Jack, glinting like Adrudian on fire. "The King found this ritual site, the House of Matchsticks. He stole the keystone—the pendant. Somehow, it ended up with your roommate." Winn gestured to Nalissa, who winced, her mouth thinning. "Now, Faraday needs it back. I don't know why, but it has something to do with his clockworks, and that ... *someone* we just heard through the lock. That *someone* who's trapped, and asking for help." She flashed them an angled smile. "Let's help them."

Neave popped her knuckles, returning Winn's smile twofold. "So, we go into the mines tomorrow. To find the House of Matchsticks—and whoever's trapped down there."

Winn stood still, chewing on the match. She didn't need to reply; the answer was already spreading through the room, through each of them. Jame nodded, then Nalissa, and Cameron.

Winn's gaze circled to Jack. "And you?"

Jack squeezed his eyes shut, then opened them again. He had told himself he'd say no. Let them go. Make an expedition himself. Find the House of Matchsticks alone.

But his silence said enough. A grin spread over

Cameron's face, brightening his clean-cut features like a beam of sunlight.

"Yes?" he prompted.

Jack dropped into his chair, rubbing his hands through his hair. He was tired enough to sink into the floor and stay there, fossilized, until the world turned to ash and dirt.

"Yes," Jack said. "I'll come."

6

THE GIRL WITH THE PENDANT

ISALINE

Cameron led the five of them out of Little Space, ducking through the door and into the bright kitchen beyond. The cooks acknowledged him silently, wiping down their cutting blocks as if there hadn't been a hurricane raging in Little Space minutes ago. Isaline stepped out behind Neave, clutching her bag and the trident close to her middle.

An empty feeling had grown in the pit of her stomach. The last hours were muddled, dreamlike, setting her mind reeling. How could her pendant, something she'd worn every day for years, hold secrets without her knowing? And if Winn was right and the lock *was* the keystone from the House of Matchsticks, how did Isaline come to have it? Before today, she'd never left Fort Upper.

Don't think about that now, she told herself, trying to remember to breathe. There were more important things to worry about, like where she was going to sleep tonight. Exhaustion weighed on her limbs, despite her whirling mind; even with all she'd learned in the past hour, she didn't think she could stay awake another night.

Beyond the kitchen, the Harper and Cup's tavern was empty, its shiny tables and chairs bathed in white moonlight. Jame and Winn emerged from the kitchen last, their heads bent together, whispering. After a nod of agreement, Jame came to stand at Isaline's side, so close she could feel the heat from his arm. She was grateful for him—his presence was an anchor, something familiar to keep her from fragmenting into pieces.

They gathered in front of the bar, arranging their belongings and doing up their coats. Winn strode to the front of the room and wrapped her face and hair with the blue scarf. Neave sidestepped past her and pushed the door of the inn open. A whoosh of air cooled Isaline's burning cheeks.

"I'll escort the Princess back to the palace," Neave said, running a hand down the silver buttons on her coat. "And pick her up tomorrow night, too, of course."

"I don't need an escort," Winn replied through her scarf.

"That's true." Neave tucked loose strands of hair behind her ears. Her weapons belt sat tight on her hips, emphasizing her tall figure next to the shorter Princess. "But I'll sleep better."

Winn didn't seem to know how to respond to that. She

tucked the ends of her scarf into her coat. "If you insist, then." Turning to pull Cameron into a hug, she said, "Tomorrow."

"Tomorrow," Cameron repeated, and Winn slipped from the tavern with Neave into the cool night.

When they were gone, Jack squeezed past Isaline and crouched behind the bar. Glass clinked, and he stood up holding a massive bottle of brandy. Isaline arched her brows as he twisted out the cork, tilted the bottle, and took a long swig.

"I'm in agreement," Jame said. He pointed at the bottle, his eyes turning into amused half-moons. "But I'm pretty sure that's for customers."

Jack slid a hand into his pocket and pressed four shiny gold pieces to the bar, still drinking. Isaline swallowed a gasp—it was more money than she'd ever seen at once. She gazed at the coins while Cameron chuckled, leaning backward against a table and adjusting his tie.

"For that much gold, you can have two bottles," he said. The moonlight washed the color from his hair, making it look flaxen. He arranged the pieces falling over his forehead. "Throw in some more, and I can sell the inn."

Jack choked on the brandy, going into a brief coughing fit. Isaline looked from the gold to Cameron, her eyes widening.

"*You're* the owner of the Harper and Cup?"

Cameron's teeth flashed white. "One of my many

titles." He brushed at his gloves, then gestured with the top of his head at a stairway leading up from the shadowed fireplace. "Speaking of which. Nalissa, Jack—I'll show you to your rooms. I had Minna make them up before you arrived."

Rooms. A tense rope in Isaline's shoulders relaxed. She was dizzy with the thought of an actual bed, instead of the forest floor or a hard train seat.

Jack scrubbed the back of his sleeve over his mouth and seized the neck of another bottle. "I can find my room myself," he muttered, trudging from behind the bar.

To Isaline's surprise, Cameron grinned suddenly, as if he'd won a hand of cards. He reached into his pocket and produced a ring of keys. Most of them were iron and plain, but there was a single shiny gold key that caught Isaline's eye. A vault key? The key to a mansion somewhere?

Jack tucked his brandy bottles behind one arm and took a plain iron key from the Head Inspector's outstretched fingers. If he noticed the flash of gold, he didn't show it; he thumped up the stairs and disappeared onto the second floor without another word.

Jame, Cameron, and Isaline listened to the creak of his boots until the sound faded.

"I like him," Jame said, giving Cameron a broad smile.

Cameron stared at the dark stairway a moment, one corner of his mouth pulling up. "I'm just happy he took the room. I was expecting him to sleep on the beach." He unlinked another iron key and held it out to Isaline.

"*You'll* allow me to be a good host, won't you? Your room's upstairs at the end of the hall. I'll show you where."

"Um ... sure." She took the key and pressed the cold metal into her palm. She'd never had a room all her own—at an inn or elsewhere—but Nalissa wouldn't have balked. Besides, Cameron had the keen look of someone who had been starved of companions with whom to be hospitable. She took a deep breath and followed him to the stairs.

As she walked by, Jame pressed his fingers lightly to her sleeve. He nodded at her, then strolled backward toward the door of the inn, his features silhouetted against the moonlit windows. She could just make out the modest tilt of his lips.

After, he mouthed to her, and Isaline understood.

Isaline's room was the last of a row of green-painted doors at the top of the stairs. Windows cast blocks of silvery light on the wooden floor, illuminating her and Cameron's way down the hall. When they had reached the right door, Cameron stood aside as Isaline turned the key in its lock. The latch opened with a *thunk*.

"Here we are," he said, and waved Isaline inside.

The room was smaller than her dorm room at Casret Academy, but more comfortable. The walls and floor were smooth, dark wood. A narrow bed sat in the far corner, across from a wooden desk, an old-looking wardrobe, and the door to a little bathroom. A round window sat above the bed, letting in a slant of moonlight.

Isaline tiptoed inside, as if afraid to disturb the room's peaceful sleep. She propped her trident on the wall and turned the dial on a lantern sitting on the desk. Orange light spilled out, pushing away the darkness.

Cameron folded his arms and leaned against the door jamb. "It'll be comfortable?"

"Yes." Isaline's fingers slid off the top of the desk as she took in the rest of the room. It was tiny and worn, but it was *hers*. She set her bag on the floor. "Thank you."

Cameron nodded, satisfied. "Rest up, Thief. See you tomorrow."

He turned to leave, but Isaline raised a hand to stop him.

"Actually, wait," she said. There had been a sliver of truth bothering her since listening to Winn's recording in Little Space. It wanted to be spoken aloud, but she hadn't figured out how to express it at the meeting. "I wanted to tell you. This pendant." She gestured to her neck, where the lock lay buried inside her collar. "It didn't belong to my roommate. It's been mine for as long as I can remember."

Cameron leaned on the door jamb again, pinning her with a curious expression. "Interesting. Why did you say it belonged to your friend?"

"I ..." Isaline walked over to the bed, skimming her fingertips over its soft, threadbare quilt. "I wanted ..."

"It's okay," Cameron said gently, after a second of watching her struggle. "I know it was a hard decision to come here. You mentioned you didn't want to leave your friend. It makes sense you would try to bring her along."

Isaline froze halfway to sitting on the bed, blinking.

Nalissa mentioned me in her letters?

Cameron didn't seem to notice the wave of surprise washing over Isaline's face. He examined the shine on the point of his boots, folding his arms closer to his chest. "I've lied before, too, to help my friends."

It's more than that, Isaline wanted to say, but she twisted her mouth closed and looked through the window. Seawater stretched beyond the glass, blending like ink into the black sky. She felt tiny, like a single grain of sand tumbling on a vast beach.

After a pause, she said, "If I've always had the pendant, then I'm the girl that monster mentioned in the recording."

Cameron nodded, running a fingertip over the sleeve of his coat. "*It is with the girl. The wearer forgets*, and all that."

"Exactly. But I can't be ... it seems like too much of a coincidence."

For a moment, Cameron considered this. Then his face broke into a practiced smile. "Quite the contrary. It's not a coincidence at all. You're meant to be here."

"What do you mean?" Less than a week ago, Isaline was a Watchling getting ready to take her Weeklong

Review. Now, everything had changed: she'd been expelled from her school, her best friend was gone, and she'd traveled across Benemourne behind Nalissa's identity. All to find out that she—not Nalissa—had been mentioned on this recording. "How could it be me?"

"Destiny," Cameron said, enunciating the word as if relishing its sound. He took one of Jack's gold coins from his pocket and flicked it, sending it flipping through the air and onto the back of his hand. "Fate's been stirring. It knows how everything connects, one to the other. It pushed you here."

Isaline sank onto the edge of her bed, her knees wobbling. Nalissa had believed in fate—they'd spoken about it on late nights, sitting side-by-side on the dormitory's rooftop—but it didn't feel like Cameron was speaking to Nalissa.

I'm here for a reason. Fate chose me.

The thought had resonance, spreading through her body like an earthquake. She tried to push it away, but it turned instead and plunged deep, planting itself in her heart, a shoot with baby-green leaves.

Cameron watched her silently, his mouth turned up in a thoughtful expression. "Whatever brought you here ..." He stood up from the wall, smoothing the ends of his Watchman's coat. "You made the right choice."

Isaline covered her throat with her hand, pressing the lock between her collarbones. "How do you know?"

He winked at her before starting down the hallway, leaving a patch of moonlight in his wake.

"Because it's the choice you made," he said.

As Cameron's footsteps faded, Isaline took a shallow breath and held it for a count of four. Her heart was racing, pounding against her ribs hard enough to make her vision pulse. She flopped backward onto the bed, clamping her eyes shut.

Before the meeting, Isaline had been determined to either escape into Ar or commit to her disguise. Now, she didn't have a choice. Nalissa's mission wasn't just Nalissa's mission anymore—it had transformed into something else.

The House of Matchsticks. The King's workshop in the mines. The lock.

Somewhere in her past, Isaline had a connection. To what, it almost didn't matter; a connection itself was more than she'd ever dreamed. Nalissa had struggled not knowing where she was from, and Isaline had hardly dared wonder about her own history. She'd assumed she was some unwanted child, cast into an orphanage after birth. But what if she wasn't? What if she was meant for something, as Cameron said?

Destiny. The word struck something curled in the cage of her ribs. She hadn't known it before, but a question had been sheltered there, sleeping all this time.

Who am I, really?

Isaline opened her eyes. For now, she was Nalissa. She had to be. If what Cameron said was true, she couldn't afford to be thrown out of the expedition, not if she wanted to know where the pendant came from. Where *she* came from. Somehow, she would have to keep fooling everyone into thinking she was a Quandary Thief.

Well, almost *everyone,* she thought, and rolled onto her knees.

Beyond the round window above her bed, the lights of bobbing boats were tiny pinpricks on the ocean. Waves crashed and smoothed against the shore, drawing close to where a figure was sitting on the sand with his legs stretched out, precisely where Isaline thought he'd be.

Drumming her fingers, Isaline stared at his silhouette until the nervous tingling in her feet wouldn't let her sit still. She shifted off the bed, tiptoed down the stairs, and stepped through the front door of the inn into the fragrant air.

She headed toward the figure sitting near the water, boots sinking into the sand. He looked up as she approached.

"Hey," she said.

"Hi," Jame responded.

She sat next to him, stretching her legs. The tide rolled toward them, not quite touching the soles of Jame's boots, which stuck out farther than hers. His toe tapped at the air.

"Want some?" Jame reached into his coat and pulled out a small silver flask. He popped open the top, smelled the contents, and shuddered. "I have no idea what it is."

"Not particularly," Isaline replied. The bitter scent of the alcohol carried on the sea breeze, stinging the inside of her nose.

Jame laughed, shaking his head. "I was hoping you'd try it so I wouldn't have to. But ..." He lifted the flask, toasting her, and took a sip. Isaline snorted as he sputtered into the back of his hand. "Oh, awful. He really does drink cheap liquor."

She studied him a moment, then a memory clicked into place. "So it *was* you," she said. Donborough's rant seemed days ago, but it had only been a few hours since Jame had confronted him in the tavern. "You stole that Watchman's flask."

"He stole it first. I have a mind to return it to its rightful owner tomorrow." Jame coughed again. "With some better liquor."

Isaline laughed, a little too loudly, and cleared her throat. There was no doubt Jame wanted to ask why she had shown up in Ar disguised as Nalissa. The thought of talking about it made her tongue stick to the roof of her mouth. She wished Nalissa hadn't said anything about Jame having a crush on her—not knowing would make speaking to him so much easier.

Jame pocketed the flask and cast her a sidelong glance. "It's weird, that thing."

Isaline paused, momentarily distracted by a trace of silver light in his hair. "What thing?"

He tipped his chin in the direction of her hands. She hadn't realized she'd tugged the pendant out of her collar and was rolling it between her fingers.

"Something's been bothering me." Jame pulled one of his legs up and rested his elbow on his knee. He looked at the pendant as if it could jump out of her hands and bite him. "That creature. In the forest. Why did it attack us by the river?"

Of all the things that should have been bothering him, it surprised Isaline he'd landed on this one. "It wanted the lock."

"That's it, though ..." He put his hand down between them, sinking his fingers into the sand. "It already had the lock. It stole the pendant during the night, remember? But it decided to kill us at the river. Why?"

Isaline stared at the starry horizon as the water's edge pulled closer to their feet. She had wondered the same thing herself, just before the creature attacked. Why wouldn't the creature just leave the forest with the pendant? Or, if it was sent to kill, like it had said, why not do it when they were sleeping? It had already crept into their clearing and lifted the chain from her neck—one squeeze of its long fingers and she'd be dead.

Jame pulled his hand from the sand, leaving a shallow imprint that nearly brushed Isaline's side. "It's just ... it hadn't been trying very hard to kill us, before the river."

"Maybe it knew *I'd* try to kill you," she said.

A twitch of laughter played across his mouth. "I'm glad you didn't."

"Me, too."

Silence fell as they listened to the churning water. Isaline rested her hand in the sand where Jame's had been, letting the cool grains come up between her fingers. She'd grown used to silence in the forest at Casret, but here, being quiet with Jame felt different. The air seemed to murmur between them, coaxing words to her mouth. She wanted to tell him about Nalissa. She wanted to thank him for keeping her secret.

But she opened her mouth and other things came tumbling out, instead.

"I've had this—the lock—for a really long time," she said. "I don't know where it came from. I wasn't planning to go on this ... trip. I wasn't planning for any of this to happen. It just kind of *happened*, and now here I am, and I feel like I have to figure this out because ..." Isaline hesitated, shrinking from the sound of her own voice. "Because if the pendant is so—what if I'm—"

"Special," Jame finished for her. He rested the side of his head in his hand and regarded her closely. The jewels on his rings poked out of his hair, twinkling red-blue-green.

"Right. Special." Isaline let the rest of the words come out as air. She slumped her shoulders, bunching the sand into a lump beneath her palm.

Jame just nodded. "Being special is overrated."

He had drawn closer to her. Isaline could feel the warmth of his hand, resting on his thigh right above her own in the sand. Her heart thumped suddenly, bringing heat to her cheeks, but Jame didn't seem to notice. His gaze roamed over her face.

"Why didn't you tell me?" he asked. His voice sounded different. It sent a flutter up the back of Isaline's arms.

"Tell you what?"

"Your name, in the forest."

Isaline bit her tongue, trying to dig up the reason. She had been a Watchling, and he was a Quandary Thief—but she wasn't a Watchling anymore, and he wasn't like the Thieves she'd been warned about at school. He planted flowers and knitted with pear-green yarn on the grass. He bought her apple cider. He kept her secret.

Isaline flattened her hand in the sand again. The tip of her little finger came up against his.

"I'm ..." she trailed off, expecting Jame to withdraw. Instead, he slid his hand onto hers, entwining their fingers. It wasn't the same as before, when their hands had skimmed against each other in the forest—this was deliberate. Her fingers curled reflexively around his, holding them.

"I'm not ..." Isaline's voice was hushed. She shivered as Jame brushed his fingers against her temple, sweeping a strand of her hair from her eyes. "I'm not very good at … talking."

"Can I kiss you, then, instead?"

She paused, then nodded, and kept nodding until he stopped her with his mouth on hers. He kissed her softly, lips barely touching, then with more pressure, and more. For a moment, all Isaline could do was notice: the way he threaded his hand through her hair, the feeling of his lips parting, the whisper of his breath against her cheek. It was *good*, better than she'd imagined it might be—and it had taken her this long to recognize she'd imagined it at all. She pulled him closer, palm sinking into the warmth at the back of his neck.

Finally, Jame pulled back and the cool touch of seawater nudged Isaline's ankles. The tide had rolled up over their boots. She pulled in her knees, pressing her thigh against Jame's arm where it reached to cup her face.

"My name is …"

"I know." Jame laughed, pressing his forehead against hers. "Nalissa."

A beat went by, and another. Isaline's mind struggled to understand what he'd said. Then a tightness covered her chest and seized her throat. She pulled her face away from Jame's. "What?"

He said it again, speaking softly still. The syllables of Nalissa's name chilled her, pressing ice to her flushed skin. Jame released her and she scooted backward on the sand. "You think my name is Nalissa?"

His brows pulled together into a frown. "It is, isn't it? Do you go by something else? You never mentioned it in—"

"The letters." Isaline's arms began to tremble. She'd thought Jame could never mistake Nalissa's voice for her own. Isaline's speech was halting, disjointed, nothing like Nalissa's graceful sentences or the musical flow of her words. But there was no hidden joke on Jame's face. His cheeks were pink, warm with their kiss, but his expression was earnest. Isaline's heart pounded. "You don't think I sound ... different? From the letters?"

Jame sat back and drew up his knees. He studied her for two long seconds, then shrugged. "I don't think so? I'm not sure what you want me to ..." His mouth fell open as Isaline stood bolt upright, brushing off her pants. "Hey, wait—"

"I need to go." Her feet carried her backward a few steps. They were freezing cold where the ocean water had drenched them. She could hardly think that a moment ago she'd thought he *knew* her—that he had known she was an imposter, and kissed her anyway.

Jame got to his feet, too, not bothering to scrape the sand from his clothes. The night was dim enough to shadow his features against the boat lights sprinkled on the sea behind him. He rubbed the back of his neck.

"I'm not sure what ..." His tone wavered and he cleared his throat. A surge of guilt made Isaline's knees lock. "Did I do something wrong?"

"No," Isaline said quickly. She backed further away from him. "I just—I have to go."

She whirled and raced toward the Harper and Cup, digging her heels into the sand. If she stayed, she would have to tell Jame the truth. Her name wasn't Nalissa. She wasn't anything *like* Nalissa—and he couldn't know that, now. If he did, he'd never keep her secret. He'd never want to talk to her again. Destiny or not, Isaline couldn't make herself into the girl he'd written to.

The Harper and Cup emerged from the darkness and Isaline doubled her pace, jogging to the green door. Before she could let herself in, Jame called to her from the beach.

"You seemed more ..." His voice had risen a note, as if he were trying to yell and whisper at the same time. Isaline rubbed a hand under her wet eyes and turned to face him again. "Honest, I guess? In the letters."

She winced. "Honest?"

Jame shook his head limply. "I don't know ... that's not the right way to say it." He hadn't followed her, but had walked a few paces so the tide had stopped running over his boots. "It's just that ... I feel like I got to know a lot about you, in those letters. But in person, I—you didn't say much. You didn't even tell me who you were, when you were on your exam."

A hand closed itself over Isaline's heart. She saw Nalissa, standing on the rooftop, leaning to the side as if to cartwheel along the thin ledge above the drop. She backed away, pressing herself against the Harper and Cup's door.

"There's someone else," she called to Jame in a shaking voice. "A boy at school. I meant to—to tell you earlier. I'm sorry."

Jame didn't respond, just stood there, lowering his shoulders. Isaline rubbed at her cheeks. She heaved open the door and latched it behind her, leaving him alone on the beach.

In her room, she closed the slats on the lantern until its orange light winked out. Sniffing, she sat on the bed, staring at the wall for minutes or hours, teasing her choices apart like so many threads. Try as she might, she couldn't find the line—the thin, invisible spider's thread—that led her to the feelings she had for Jame. She wanted to yank it free, examine it, change it.

Fate has been stirring. Cameron's voice came back to her, ringing in her ears. *It knows how everything connects, one to the other.*

Later, before she drifted into sleep, Isaline pressed her pendant between two fingers and prayed to whoever had given it to her, like she had done so many times before.

7

THE DARK PALACE
THE COLLECTOR

After the meeting, Winn and Neave ignored the usual route back into Ar and cut across the beach instead, coming right to the base of the Watch Wall. There, painted lily-white to blend in with the marble, was the tallest ladder the Collector had ever seen. At first, it appeared Neave and Winn had simply climbed into the air, the ladder was so well hidden—but when he and Caladrius stood at its base, its shape discerned itself against the night sky.

The Collector followed the ladder with his eyes all the way to the crest of the Wall, rungs receding into the distance like train tracks standing up. Caladrius tweeted, jumping onto the ladder and gazing down at him.

"All right, Cal," he said and climbed after Neave and Winn.

He soon cleared the low buildings at the base of the

Wall and the sea spread out behind him, glimmering. The Collector's arms grew heavy as he climbed, seizing him with a sudden panic. Were his arms *tired*? What could it mean, his limbs growing fatigued like a human's did? Could it be from lack of air—a strange symptom of his growing urge to breathe? The urge had stayed with him even after he had fled the Harper and Cup. Even after he left Isaline behind.

Take a breath.

The exhaustion must be an illusion, a trick of the night. If he was tired, the Collector surmised, it had come instead over the course of the evening, standing and watching in Little Space. Letting time slip away while souls stay safe in the chests of the living.

Their plan to break into the mines unnerved him. The Collector had descended into the mines only once, after the fire at the Adrudian mill sixteen years ago. He had stooped in the narrow tunnels, collecting the souls of pick-axer after pickaxer, their bodies burned to black husks. Before long, an unnamable fear coursed through him, tightening his throat into a fist. He felt as if he had been there before, and seen a coiled, eyeless thing waiting for him in the dark.

He had emerged hoping to never return.

The Collector shook his head, pushing away the memory. *Déjà vu, that's all it was.* He stopped climbing and hooked his elbows around the ladder's sides, bracing his feet against the rungs. Caladrius twittered from her perch above him. He craned and shot her a hard look, watching as she flitted to and fro, both darker and brighter than the night.

"I need a moment." The Jar of Lights, hanging over his elbow, clattered against the bars of the ladder. He gazed down to the beach below, small enough to hold in the palm of his hand. "Oh, stars, we're far away from the ground."

Caladrius chirped, as if to say, *We're losing them.*

"I know, I know, Cal." The Collector gulped, clamping his mouth closed against the air that pressed at his lips. "We don't all have wings."

Winn and Neave were some ways above them, scuttling up the ladder like beetles, steadying themselves against the high air's breeze. The Collector's hands drank the moonlight.

Maybe this expedition is a good thing, he thought. Maybe Isaline would die underground, setting right his mistake. Things could go back to the way they were. He and Caladrius could return to collecting the souls of the dead. They could pretend they had never known about these humans, and would never have to know what was waiting at the end of this strange path.

But that's a lie, the Collector's mind whispered. *Caladrius knows. The Justs told her. They told her, and now she wants to show you.*

Take a breath.

The ladder shuddered as Winn and Neave came to a halt above. They were breathing hard, their breaths fracturing in the air as curls of steam. Winn's soft, raspy voice fell through the night's silence.

"... could find my own way." The Princess was three or four rungs behind Neave, pressed tight to the ladder with the heels of her leather boots pressed against its sides. "I know where I'm going."

Neave gave a good-natured tut. She grinned down at Winn, past the black coattails the wind gathered against her thighs. "You've got more grit than I imagined you would, Princess, but everyone in this city wants a piece of you. You're the King's engineer, right? Even Ar's stuffiest scholars would corner you trying to get information about his clockworks."

Winn considered this for a moment, then said, "I could handle it."

"I've no doubt about that."

"I was in hiding for years, don't forget."

Neave's flashlight swung as she repositioned herself on the ladder. "I couldn't forget. You and my family have that in common."

"Your family," Winn said. "They were—"

"Spies, actually." The ladder trembled as Neave started to climb again. "They were both Country Watch, until they started spying for the Quandary." She grunted, heaving herself upwards. "Not the safest job, as you probably know."

Winn tugged her scarf over her hair and climbed up after Neave. "What happened to them?"

"Oh, they're still alive somewhere. The Watch will catch up to them eventually. I didn't care to find out when *eventually* was coming."

A quiet minute stretched out between them. When Winn spoke again, her voice was low.

"I'd give anything to be with my parents right now."

Neave glanced down at her. "I know. Are they okay?"

"They're hiding away from the city. I left them to ... to do this. When I was studying to be part of the Seven Thrones, Lillian and Philip looked after me. My parents and I would visit them when I was a kid. They were good people."

"I know." Neave stopped again, letting the sound of the breeze rush into the space where her next footfall would have been. "When I came here, I wanted more than anything to be a Treasurehunter. Lillian and Philip let me use their library."

Winn's boot came down hard on a rung, making the ladder vibrate. "They let you read their books, too?"

"They did." Neave's eyes shone in the edges of her flashlight's beam. "They *were* good people. Gave me a chance when I had none, and I never got an opportunity to thank them."

"Well, they made their choice." Winn clutched the ladder, steadying her shaking arms. Her powder-blue skirts billowed in the breeze. "They knew what they were sacrificing."

Neave nodded and folded her braid around her

shoulders. Beyond her head, the top of the Wall rose out of the darkness. They were almost there, a thought that made the Collector dizzy with relief. Caladrius nudged his nose with her beak before hopping up to the next rung.

"It's strange we didn't meet, if your family knew Lillian and Philip," Neave said after a moment.

"Maybe we did. How many years ago?"

"I was young. Thirteen. I met ..." Neave blew out her breath as she climbed another rung. "I met a boy who would come to the library sometimes, but I never met a girl."

A beat passed, then Winn replied, "So, we did meet. That was me." She looked briefly at the soles of Neave's boots. "It's just, at the time, no one realized I was a girl. Until I told them."

The quality of the darkness above Neave had changed; she was nearly at the top of the Wall. Still, she stopped and gave Winn a quick nod. "I see. Well, it's nice to finally meet you, Winn."

"You too."

They fell into silence as they climbed the last stretch of ladder. Neave pulled herself up the last rung and peeked over the top of the Wall.

"No one around, at least that I can see." She glanced down at Winn. "You okay in the dark?"

"The moon's bright enough," Winn said, but Neave had already heaved herself up over the side. Her head appeared again a moment later, the length of her braid swinging in the air. She stretched out her hand to Winn.

"Up we go," she said.

Winn grasped Neave's hand and clambered over the Wall's side. The iron ladder shook, free of climbers save for the Collector and Caladrius, who weighed nothing at all. The Collector heaved himself up a moment later and rolled over the edge, keeping away from where Neave and Winn lay panting.

"Your hands are soft, for a Treasurehunter," Winn said, leaning her head back against the cool stone.

Neave laughed, a sudden bark that echoed through the empty streets of Ar spread out before them.

"It's been a while," she said.

NEAVE AND WINN took a short route through Ar's narrow alleyways toward the palace square. They side-stepped buildings and edged around domes of orange light shining from doorways. The Collector and Caladrius followed, skimming over the greasy street and swallowing the moonlight that edged between rooftops above.

The Collector's arms had lightened since leaving the ladder behind, but his heart grew heavier all the time. Caladrius was twittering, even *singing* as they shadowed Neave and Winn up to the rooftop of a tall building. He wanted to cage her in his palms and carry her away somewhere safe. But it wouldn't be right—she had always done the leading. The carrying.

Neave crouched on the rooftop, gazing out over the cobblestone road below.

"Any second, now." She unclipped a pair of brass binoculars from her weapons belt and peered into the darkness of the street. "With any luck, we'll be the only travelers tonight."

Winn pulled the strap of her bag over her head, switching shoulders. "It's getting too dark for normal folk at night." She gazed up at the spread of twinkling buildings above them, a thousand pinpricks of light winding up the face of the mountain. "They'd rather stay inside. Use their Adrudian indoors."

Neave smirked and tapped the brass of her binoculars with a long, black-tipped nail. "Fat lot of good that will do them." A clattering sound and the rumble of wheels emerged from the end of the street, getting steadily louder. Neave got to her feet, offering a hand to Winn. "Here it is. Want me to count down?"

The Collector peered into the shadows below and the shape of an empty, driverless trolley materialized, shaking forward along its track set into the cobblestone street. Caladrius chirped. It was going to pass directly beneath them.

Winn tightened the scarf around her head and repositioned the strap of her bag on her shoulder. "Count down? Hardly."

The trolley lurched up beneath the building and Winn leaped, sailing down in a plume of skirts to land on top of the trolley's roof. Neave drew a surprised breath.

"Impressive," she whispered to herself, and leaped after Winn.

The Collector drifted down behind them, holding the brim of his hat in one hand and the Jar of Lights in the other. Neave and Winn sat cross-legged atop the trolley's clattering roof, staring silently at the city as it rolled by like a strip of painted paper. Sparkling ocean and cliffs peeked between the buildings at intervals, offering brief images awash in moonlight. The Collector stood at the other end of the trolley, picking at his sleeves.

When the palace square came into view, Neave hopped down from the trolley's roof onto the glistening street. Winn followed, dropping heavily and waving her arms to keep her balance. Neave reached out and steadied her.

"See? Good thing I took you all this way." Neave extracted her hand from the bundle of Winn's scarf. "You could have fallen right there."

The small bridge of Winn's nose wrinkled, the hint of a smile hiding. "Guess so."

They turned toward the moonlit road, staring at the place where it opened into the palace's flat, black-tiled square. The palace itself rose like an obsidian giant against the peaks of other mountains in the distance. The

Collector could just see the silhouette of King Faraday's crimson-sailed airship sitting near the door.

Winn's smile fell, her features tightening. She curled her fingers around the strap of her bag. "You taking me all *that* way?"

Neave's teeth flashed in a quick grin. "Clockwork guards make me uncomfortable."

"As they should." Winn tugged down the front of her scarf, nodding at Neave through the darkness. "Thank you. I will see you again."

The weapons in Neave's belt clanked together as she leaned forward in a low bow. She swept her arm to the side, flourishing. "You will. Be safe, Princess."

They parted ways. The sound of Neave's boots disappeared around a corner, and Winn's shorter strides took her toward the palace. The Collector's ribs constricted. Caladrius had settled near his chin, claws gripping the fabric of his coat, and he knew which way she wanted him to go. The massive obsidian palace cast shadows that reached out for the tips of his boots.

"There's a strange feeling I get," the Collector said, shifting and shifting his grip on the Jar of Lights, "when I look at that place."

Take a breath.

Caladrius whistled, sharing the shiver that walked across the Collector's shoulders. She wasn't flying ahead of him this time. Her claws squeezed, bunching his coat. The

Collector grew cold with the realization that she, too, was afraid.

Down the street, Winn's footsteps were soft over the blank tile of the palace square. The silence set every nerve in the Collector's body twanging, telling him to flee in the other direction. To get away from this place.

Caladrius whistled again, so low it was almost a whisper. He knew she wouldn't give him a choice.

The Collector flattened his hat on his head, trained his eyes on the dark mass before him, and walked after Winn.

THE HEELS of Winn's boots beat a barely perceptible rhythm through the night's quiet. The Collector and Caladrius trailed after her, peering at a line of clockwork guards in front of the towering, tar-black doors of the palace. They were silent, long-armed, big enough to lift an intruder up by their neck and crunch their bones. As Winn approached, they turned their heads in tandem toward her, wood sliding on metal. Winn didn't falter under the weight of their combined gaze.

"*Theresa*," she said to them. "Stand down."

The clockworks slid their heads back to position. Caladrius chirped softly, but the Collector couldn't find words to respond. *Theresa*. That had been the name of the woman Faraday had killed in the boat, hadn't it? What did it mean, that he had used her name as the password?

Winn heaved the door and swung it open, letting out a whoosh of stale air, as if the building were a crypt instead of a royal palace. The Collector watched as the Princess slipped into the crack of darkness beyond, tiny against the huge door like a mouse scuttling under a wall. Caladrius cooed, going stone-still on his shoulder.

"Are you sure about this?" he asked her. His hands had gone clammy, sweat beading inside his gloves. The crack of darkness beyond the door shrank as it swung slowly closed, an eye winking. "This feels—"

Caladrius tightened her claws. He stared at her, his stomach wrapping itself into a knot, but there wasn't anything else to say.

The Collector raised the Jar of Lights and melted through the thick obsidian door and into the chamber beyond. It was pitch-black and dry inside the palace, a marked change from the grease-thick air outside. The Collector squinted into the darkness, swinging the Jar of Lights around in a circle and finding nothing but a thick layer of dust coating the marble floor. Winn's boot prints led all the way to the back, up a set of grand stone steps so smeared with grime the Collector's shoulders recoiled.

The Princess had climbed to the top of the staircase and had paused to unwrap her scarf. The Collector drifted beside her and passed the Jar of Lights into his other hand, throwing blue light down a long hallway of gilded marble. Caladrius trilled, intoning a question.

"She's lived here before, Cal," the Collector replied.

He peered at Winn's enlarged pupils in the darkness. Her face was drawn together as if she'd swallowed something sour. "She doesn't need light to find her way."

Drawing a long breath, Winn pressed her fingertips to the smooth wall of the hallway and strode forward. The Collector trailed behind. There were long tracks in the dust where Winn's fingers slid, as if she'd walked down this hallway in the dark many times before. A row of empty, rusted-over Adrudian lanterns hung above her finger tracks. The Collector lifted the Jar of Lights, letting blue light slide over the lanterns' glass and metal. They were neglected, old. The palace had long been bathed in darkness and dust.

"There are no living people here anymore," the Collector whispered, hoping the sound of his own voice would quell the rush of dread rising in his chest. Faded squares emerged out of the darkness—places where portraits of the past Seven Thrones had once hung. Name placards were still mounted in the stone beneath them: *Winn Just, Philip Just, Lillian Just, Sofia Just.* His eyes lingered on *Daniel Just* before he had to look away. "The clockworks Faraday invented don't need light to see."

They climbed up another dirt-ridden staircase, then turned down a hallway with a lit, open doorway on its left side. Amber light spilled from the doorway over the palace's smeared tiles, illuminating long streaks in the dust on the floor. It looked as if something big had been dragged along the ground.

The Collector chewed on his bottom lip. He knew this doorway. It led to the throne room, where Justs had once sat together at their seven thrones. Though Justs weren't related by blood, they shared the habit of dying peacefully within the palace walls. He and Caladrius had visited the palace on many such errands before Faraday had taken Ar.

Approaching the throne room, Winn lifted her heels and tiptoed along the wall farthest from the door, trying to stay out of sight. Despite his invisibility, the Collector mimicked her movements, pressing himself against the wall. Deep, drumming engine beats pulsed through the air. There was no way for Winn to continue down the hallway without passing by the open door. The King would see her.

Winn tried to keep to the shadows, darting around the pool of light's edge, but it was no use.

"Winn," came Faraday's voice floating into the hallway.

She froze like a Quandary Thief caught with a bag of gold. The Collector's pulse quickened. Winn wrung her hands into her skirts and backed into the light, squinting into the throne room.

"Yes?" she said.

"Come in."

The Collector followed her, looking over the top of her head. Caladrius ruffled her wings and tucked herself under his jaw, a ball of warmth where his neck met his collar.

The throne room was an immense space with vaulted windows and lines of thick pillars standing like sentinels before the King's throne. In the past, there had been the grand, ornate Seven Thrones, but now there was just one throne—jet black and high-backed with red velvet draping each side. On it sat King Faraday, his hulking body poised at the very edge of the seat like a viper curling off a branch. He had taken off one of his boots and was tipping a stream of coppery, viscous Adrudian Milk out onto the floor. His bare toes flexed, Milk dripping and sliding off his heel.

"Wait there, Winn, while I finish this business," Faraday said, gesturing with his brass chin to the base of the throne, where a man in City Watch uniform kneeled. The Watchman had his head bent, but the Collector recognized the white gloves folded on his knee. Donborough—the man who had stumbled into the alley next to the Harper and Cup.

Faraday ran a brass finger around the inside of his boot, scooping out Adrudian Milk and flicking it to the floor. "You've proven to be useful," he said to Donborough. His silver-black tongue rested on his bottom lip, wetting the pink flesh beneath his iron teeth. "Go and reassign your duties."

Donborough kept his head lowered, averting his eyes from the King. "Thank you, Your Highness." He stood up and nearly slipped in the Adrudian Milk covering the floor. It ran down the calf of his trousers where he had been kneeling in it. "I'm so pleased I—"

Faraday flicked his index finger and a spray of droplets speckled Donborough's face. "Go."

Donborough flinched, grimacing, then spun on the spot and marched back toward the door. He dragged his sleeve across his mouth as he passed Winn.

"Watchmen are tiresome," Faraday said, replacing his boot. His breaths rumbled and shook with the engine in his chest. "Clockworks are much easier to manage. Don't you agree?"

Winn approached the throne with her shoulders squared, careful to avoid the pool of Milk on the floor. She dropped to one knee in a low bow. "Good evening, Highness."

"Good evening, indeed." Faraday studied her, one bloodshot eye dragging up and down her body. His sharp gaze made the Collector's arms tremble. "Your absence hurts me. Ar is not so friendly at night."

Winn tucked her bag over her shoulder as she stood again. Her eyes had darkened to the point of blackness, as if drawing back into her head. "My business in the city—it took longer than anticipated. The trolley you sent me to fix proved difficult."

"You're an engineer, not a servant." Faraday wiped his fingers on a swathe of red velvet. Long streaks of dried Milk thickened the fabric. He drew back his lips. "Engineers can return before the job is done."

Winn took a tiny step backward, nearly bumping the Collector and Caladrius. "I'm sorry, sir."

Faraday paused, considering her, then rocked back against the throne and crossed his arms. Brass clanked on brass. He tapped his fingertip to his chin. *Tap-tap-tap.*

Take-a-breath.

The Collector's lungs contracted. He swallowed, locking his mouth. Caladrius tittered.

"Perhaps you need a reminder of what will become of you, Winn, if you disappear again." Faraday's sunken eyes narrowed to slits. *Tap-tap-tap.* "It is a worse fate than what befell your friends at the Seven Thrones."

Winn's mouth shut tight into a hard line. She took another step backward, shuffling on the dusty floor. The Collector moved around to her side, watching as the corners of Faraday's mouth tilted up, his cheeks wrinkling against brass.

"Richard," Faraday called, turning to look over his shoulder. "Why don't you come out now?"

A patch of shadows detached itself from the far corner of the room. There was a sound like someone dragging a heavy sack across the floor. The back of the Collector's neck prickled, and Winn visibly shivered, eyes widening.

"That's ... it's ..." She wound her hands into her skirts as the man-snake from the forest at Casret Academy slid into the light, its clammy body curling like a centipede. It slithered to the throne's side and coiled itself up, lifting its face and letting its head loll onto its pale shoulder. Winn stared at the two squirming lumps beneath its blindfold, at the ruined nostrils flapping with its breath. "Did you call it *Richard*?"

Faraday's grin widened. "That was his name before." He looked at the monster fondly, as if it were a rare sculpture on display. His fingertips skimmed the crown of Richard's head amid sparse patches of colorless hair. "Years ago, I made Richard into what he is now. And you, Winn ..." The King leaned forward, bringing his face inches from Winn's. "I can *make* you, too."

Winn swallowed. Her upper lip trembled, but she didn't shrink back. She met the King's gaze with a strong and steady look. "I understand, Highness," she said. Her eyes flicked to the monster, gaze looping up its body.

"Good." Faraday blinked, his smile knitting closed. He leaned back against the throne again and resumed *tap-tap-tapping* his chin with his brass finger. "You may go."

"Thank you." The words flew out of Winn's mouth, deflating her chest. She backed away from the King. "Goodnight."

"Goodnight, Winn."

The Collector watched her stride from the throne room.

Take a breath.

The urge to breathe had worsened beyond anything he'd felt before. Fire raged in his chest, licking his ribcage. He turned to follow Winn, but Caladrius whistled loudly in his ear, stopping him short.

"I can't stay here much longer," the Collector said to her. His voice was shaky and weak.

Faraday turned to Richard, pulling a long breath, then letting it out against the rumble of his engine. "She and her friends mean to stop me," he said. *Tap-tap-tap.* "The way you did, all those years ago. You, and Mio, and Haris ... and Theresa."

A cold shiver climbed the Collector's spine, sticking pins into his shriveling lungs. Faraday stared into the darkness behind the vaulted windows.

"Go after the pendant," he said finally. "I'll send orders for the mill to be closed. We'll give them a little head start, shall we?"

Richard made a sound like a dying winter wind, breathy and groaning. He uncoiled and slithered past the Collector. Caladrius chirped, digging her claws into his shoulder.

"He knows, Cal," the Collector whispered. "He knows where they're going. They're all going to die."

The pressure inside his chest was turning him inside out. Caladrius chirped again, but the Collector could hardly hear her—a painful, rising warmth was spreading through his body. Moaning, he covered his mouth with his hand.

Take a breath.

Take a breath, take a breath, take a breath ...

The urge was too strong.

Squeezing his fists, the Collector opened his mouth. A

thimble of oxygen rushed past his lips, freezing his teeth in his gums and slipping down into his lungs. There, it unfurled like an opening flower, cooling the dark fire that burned in his chest, until his eyes clouded over and—

—the air gifted him a memory.

He felt himself in the past. Stuck down in the world. Existing, *not as the stars, nor as the wind, but as a body.*

A body that moved. He walked around the edge of a great, dead tree.

A body that saw. He looked back at two others, a little one. A family.

A warm body. He felt blood in his face. Real, human blood.

Faraday stopped tapping. Lost in the haze of the memory—the first memory he ever had—the Collector half-saw the King lift his head. He looked straight at the Collector.

"Hello," he said.

The memory went still, returning the Collector to the present. Confusion fuzzed his vision. Caladrius whimpered.

"Nice bird you have there." Faraday's voice was low, crawling.

The Collector choked. He clamped his hand over his throat. The King couldn't be looking at him and Caladrius, and *seeing* them, as if they were substantial. As if they were corporeal. Human.

The Collector looked down at himself. His body was a

silhouette, a shadow filled with winking stars, but he was no longer a cutout. He saw the light slide over the hem of his pants. He saw the contours of his shoes. He didn't understand his memory—he didn't understand what a memory *was*—but four words echoed in his brain, over and over.

I was a man.

I am *a man.*

Ice flooded his insides. He looked up into Faraday's eyes and it was like being peeled, the Collector's layers stripped and stripped.

Faraday leaned forward, whispering. "Haven't I seen you ... somewhere before?"

Caladrius' shrieks registered in the Collector's mind as if coming from underwater. She stabbed her beak into his earlobe, and his body jolted. He clapped a hand to the top of his hat. He clutched the Jar of Lights to his chest.

The Collector ran.

8

MORNING AND NIGHT

JACK

Jack awoke the next morning on his bed, fully clothed and drenched in cold sweat. His skull felt like it had been filled with concrete. It throbbed. He pried open his eyes, and the first thing he saw was his flask, sitting on the desk next to a dark lantern. A drip of coppery liquid spilled over the side.

Adrudian Milk. Had he Drunk last night?

Leaning against the covers of his bed, Jack groaned and rubbed his hands over his scruffy cheeks. He recalled the meeting in Little Space with vivid clarity: Winn's talking copper box, his map of the Shute, the coal-black eye behind the lock.

Cameron's smile as he agreed to go with them into the mines.

Then what?

He remembered swallowing mouthfuls of burning

brandy, tramping upstairs, and tossing himself backward onto his room's tiny bed. There, he drank from the brandy until his body grew heavy and his head lightened. He'd wished he had his notebook. The evening had stuffed his brain full, and there had been nowhere for his thoughts to go except round and round in his head.

Not long after, there had been a knock on the door.

Jack remembered opening his eyes and the ceiling wobbling, the brandy sloshing in his veins. He had paused for a second to reach a kind of equilibrium before croaking out, "Come in."

The door had cracked open, and a blond head appeared.

"Getting settled?" Cameron asked.

Jack, flat on his back on the bed, rolled his head and gave him a dull stare. Cameron had let out the kind of laugh that could have been pity or commiseration. Jack was too exhausted to tell.

"Good." Cameron had lingered in the doorway, eyes roaming the room. The space was minuscule but practical, not unlike Jack's own apartment in Lower Village. Jack slowly blinked as Cameron's gaze swept over the bottle of brandy hanging from his fingers, half-gone, then settled on the second bottle, sitting unopened on the table next to the glowing lantern.

The moment had stretched thin. Even through the buzz of alcohol, Jack could tell Cameron wasn't going to leave without being prompted. He'd heaved a sigh, pushing himself up to sitting. The room tilted, but found its way back to center—he wasn't drunk, just getting close. He'd gestured with the top of his head toward the brandy.

"Have some, then."

Cameron had paused, then swung the door open wider, admitting a shaft of moonlight. "I'll have a drink, if you insist," he said, as if Jack had insisted on anything.

He'd stepped inside, all prim posture, bright eyes, and ivory smile—but Jack knew better. Cameron had looked as tired as Jack felt. His cheeks were drawn, and one shoulder was higher than the other, as if his left arm had given up sitting as tall as his right. He'd pulled the chair out from under the desk and eased into it, knees popping. Jack reached to pass him the unopened brandy, but Cameron slipped the half-empty bottle from Jack's fingers instead. He'd lifted it to his lips, taking a long drink.

Jack leaned back on his hands, watching the brandy slosh. He couldn't find the energy to be annoyed. His mind was whirling. Had he really spoken to a woman in the mines tonight, with eyes black and round as discs? Had he *really* seen flashes of the lost expedition, or had he hallucinated, gone momentarily insane?

No. The vision had been cold and peculiar, like a dream at the edge of waking up, but it had been *real*. Jack could feel it beneath his bones. He could hear it inside his skull—the woman's strange, bisected voice intoning:

Keep this a secret, won't you?

Cameron had taken another swig from the brandy.

The bottle warped and refracted the hazy orange light, offering a bent image of the room beyond, walls stretched into shapelessness. Jack pressed his lips closed. An hour ago, *keep this a secret* had seemed easy. Natural. But now, watching Cameron's hands grip the brandy, he was surprised to find the story crouched at the back of his mouth, ready to spring forward.

Cameron had slid one eye open and smiled against the mouth of the bottle. "What?"

Jack shook his head, scrubbing his palms on the quilt beneath him. It was the brandy, that was all. It had loosened his tongue.

"Never seen you drink," he'd said.

"No one sees me drink." Cameron handed him the bottle and slumped against the back of the chair, rubbing circles into his temples. "I'm the Head Inspector."

Jack had surveyed him, taking in the midnight-black coat, the loosened tie, the glittering cufflinks. It was an old man's suit, but tonight, around the table, Cameron had seemed young.

"You don't *look* like the Head Inspector." Jack wasn't sure if it was a dig, or the truth. "It doesn't suit you."

Cameron had laughed flatly, running his fingers over the space where his badge should have been. "Honestly? Don't feel like him, either."

Jack fiddled with the ends of his own jacket, the same leather he'd been wearing since Fort Upper. Cameron didn't look like the Head Inspector, and Jack didn't look like a mill worker; his sleeves hid the burns and scars on his forearms. He didn't look like a proper Adrudian Drinker, either. And even though he was wearing a Treasurehunter's jacket, he didn't *feel* like a Treasurehunter. Not anymore.

Some part of Jack had wanted to tell Cameron this, but he'd drowned the thought in another drink instead.

"So, why'd you stop?" Jack had asked, ignoring the alcohol's burn in his throat. "Treasurehunting."

Cameron had ground the heel of his boot into the wooden floor, his shiny pointed toe swiveling. For a moment, Jack thought he wouldn't respond, but then he shrugged.

"The House of Matchsticks. The expedition. What happened to us was just *gone*, but it wasn't meant to be gone." He'd kept his eyes down, searching the floor. "The hole it left ... bled everything else dry."

Bled everything else dry.

The phrase sparked familiarity in Jack, making his stomach toss. Some memories were meant to be lost, weren't they? Jack couldn't conjure the faces of his parents, or the name of the ship that had taken them when he was young. He couldn't remember where he'd first heard about Treasurehunting. He couldn't recall what he had said to Lillian and Philip Just to make them trust him.

Memory was slippery, sure, but it wasn't meant to be *gone*. The faces of his parents had faded, and the words he'd said to the Justs had dissolved—but the expedition had been torn from him. It had been ripped away, leaving a barb behind, a parasite that drained him of feeling until he was empty. The *pull.*

Jack had peered at Cameron's eyelashes, his neatly-scrubbed skin. The Head Inspector might be pompous and false, but they had been bitten by the same thing. They had been bled. Both of them, not just one. Together.

Maybe it was the brandy, or the exhaustion, or maybe Jack had been caught up in some other, newer current, but he couldn't bring himself to lie. Taking another drink, he'd passed the bottle to Cameron.

"On the train from Fort Upper," he said, "I had a vision."

Cameron had listened as Jack recounted what he'd seen, both on the train and in Little Space. Jack had never known Cameron to be so quiet, or his eyes to be so vivid. They looked liquid, two copper pools. When Jack had described the final flash of the expedition he'd seen —*Cameron, raised off the ground with his arms hanging, a tearing sound, a gurgle, a streak of blood*—Cameron's eyes had widened, flaring with a fleeting, unreadable expression.

"Is that what happened, then?" he'd asked in a small voice. "To my chest?"

Jack nodded, making the world quiver at its edges. The bottle in Cameron's hands was empty, and Jack was a good deal drunker than he had been before he started talking. "I didn't see *how* it happened, but I saw it happen," he'd said.

They were quiet for a moment, silence weighing down the air. Jack nested his numb fingers in his lap. Cameron's injury was the only tangible clue they had been attacked in the Shute that night: something had clawed him across the chest, leaving behind a deep, raking gash. Since then, Jack had harbored a secret dread that *he* was responsible for the attack—that on the expedition Cameron had said something, or Jack had done something, and a fight had broken out. But that story didn't add up. The cut was vicious, an attempt at murder, and Jack was no killer.

He'd swallowed, dryness creeping into his mouth. He didn't *think* he was a killer.

Cameron had drawn a long breath, chest lifting. The movement caught and held Jack's gaze. He had never seen the scar, but he could *hear* it, sometimes, when Cameron stood close to him. The whisper of violence between them. The evidence of lost time, a lost moment. A lost touch.

Jack's fingers shivered. Before he knew what he was doing, he'd been reaching toward Cameron. He took the stiff fabric of Cameron's collar between index finger and thumb. He half-hoped Cameron would stop him, but he didn't, just raised his chin to give Jack's hand room. Jack had pulled the collar gently back from Cameron's neck.

There it was, on the right side—the beginnings of a long, knotted strip of flesh cutting into Cameron's collarbone. Jack's vision was swimming, but he knew the scar extended all the way down Cameron's chest, nearly to his left hip. He followed the imagined path of it with his eyes, and an image surfaced: the gash wide open, gushing warm blood, sticking Cameron's shirt to his chest as they escaped ...

The memory stopped, disintegrating. Jack dropped his hand.

"We can't—" Cameron's breath came out in a rush; he'd been holding it. He cleared his throat. "We can't tell Nalissa about the vision. She's scared enough." He'd pulled his collar closed, hiding the scar. "But we have to look after her. She could be in danger."

"Right," Jack murmured. The brandy had been catching up to him; his mind had taken on the weight of his body. He stretched his fingers.

Cameron had stood up and adjusted his tie, then his coat, then his tie again. "I don't think you should Drink Adrudian, either. It's not safe." He'd tucked a piece of hair behind his ear, face gone ashen. "We don't know what *she* wants, not really."

Jack's eyelids had grown lazy, but he'd managed to pin Cameron with a glare. "What are you talking about? It's the only way she'll show me the expedition. Some secrets shouldn't stay secret."

"Promise me you won't Drink," Cameron had said. His voice had taken on an urgency, and his eyes had lost their glimmer. He'd stood there, fiddling with something in his pocket. It must have been his ring of keys, because it let out an irritating jangle. "Say you won't Drink Adrudian. Not a drop."

Jack had looked him up and down, then shifted on his bed and eased onto his back. "You're not thinking straight."

"I am, I'm just—"

But Jack was already asleep.

HAVING RELIVED the evening in his head, Jack rolled over on his side, hunching his back against the sunlight pouring in through the window. He shouldn't have told Cameron about the visions, that was clear. At the mention of Drinking to uncover the expedition, Cameron's face had gone bloodless. Panicked. Jack didn't love the thought of being under the Head Inspector's microscope.

Then there was Cameron's chest. Jack could still feel it, rough and knotted, beneath his fingertips. The murmur of past violence between them had been as unreachable as the expedition itself. Jack couldn't believe he'd drunkenly grazed his fingers over the scar. Worse, Cameron had *let* him.

He groaned, pushing himself off the bed. For a moment, it seemed his legs wouldn't support the weight of his pounding head. Still, it was just a hangover—out of all his memories of the night before, none of them involved him Drinking Adrudian.

Why, then, was his flask sitting open on his desk, filled with Adrudian Milk?

He trudged across the room and picked up the flask. It was full to the brim. He regarded it closely, then peered into the slats of his lantern. Empty—no wonder it was emitting no light. Someone had burned the Adrudian inside to make him a drink.

Had it been Cameron, as some kind of truce? Or Jack himself, drunk and defiant in the middle of the night? No —neither made sense.

Sighing, Jack screwed the flask closed and dropped it on his bed. It didn't matter. Whoever it was, he now had a supply of Milk to bring on their expedition. Not that he would need it, being in an Adrudian mine, but Jack didn't plan to do what he was told. He hadn't promised anything. He was going to recover the lost expedition with or without Cameron's permission.

By the time Jack descended the stairs into the Harper and Cup's bustling tavern, his headache had subsided some, leaving a muffled jitter behind. Tavern patrons were packed at the wooden tables, dipping spoons into steaming bowls and gulping from overflowing goblets. Jack checked his watch—it was late afternoon. He'd slept most of the day.

None of the bar hands looked up as he sidestepped between tables and pushed through the double doors that led to the Harper and Cup's kitchen. Inside, Minna was bent over the cook's table, her silvery hair bound in a tight knot at the back of her head. She busied herself arranging a platter of bread, cheese, and some kind of grilled vegetable Jack didn't recognize. The food smelled earthy and salty. His empty stomach contracted.

"About time you showed up," Minna said to him, flashing him a smile. Jack smiled back, but the expression felt wrong on his face. "Bring this in, won't you?"

She thrust the platter of food into his arms and hurried out of the kitchen, wiping her hands on her apron. Jack stood frozen for a moment, feeling immensely awkward in the busy kitchen, then heaved the platter against his middle and backed through the open door to Little Space.

The noise of the kitchen receded as he stepped inside, replaced with the hum of voices. Afternoon sun gathered against the juniper curtains, washing everything in green-tinged light. Neave, Nalissa, and Jame were standing around the long table, speaking softly to each other. Jack shuffled over and set Minna's platter down, swiping a piece of bread and pulling out the nearest chair.

"Finally," Neave said, one hand diving toward the cheese. She had changed into clothes more suited for an expedition—a fitted black top, sturdy pants, and boots with laces up to her knees. "You'd think he'd feed us more, considering we're going—" Chewing, Neave paused, catching sight of Jack. Her lined eyes widened. "You look *terrible*."

Jack responded with a huff. "Thanks."

Both Jame and Nalissa regarded him, eyes running over his tangled hair. It had taken Jack so long to drag a comb through the knots that he had given up and pulled the top half of his hair behind his head. On his face, his broken nose had settled, but the bruise was darker and bluer than yesterday, a match for the veins reaching up the sides of his cheeks. Jack ran his palm over his jaw. He missed his usual layer of grime and soot from the mill. Without it, his face felt naked.

Lucky for him, Neave, Jame, and Nalissa didn't press questions. One by one, their attention shifted to the table's contents: a mountain of gear strewn haphazardly in a pile.

Jack inspected the gear from his chair, his brow rising. Neave must have cashed in favors with every Treasurehunter in their circle. On the table were six belted backpacks, each with basic rappelling equipment, waterskins, and black Pickaxer's headlamps with Adrudian bulbs on the front. On the other side of the piles, nearest Jack, was Treasurehunting equipment: weapons belts with Flash Cameras, binoculars, collections of short knives, thick-haired dust brushes, waterproof matches, and ...

"Are those fireworks?" Jack asked.

"I paid a visit to the Captain," Neave said with an impish grin. "Good for a distraction if we need one."

Jack nudged the band of a weapons belt to the side, examining a pistol-shaped firework with a trigger at the end. He shook his head, biting the end off his bread. Last time Jack had lit a firework, he and Cameron had nearly sent Captain Knots' wretched ferry to the bottom of the sea. He could still see the exploding fireballs ricocheting around the cabin, threatening to take Jack's legs or Cameron's arms with them.

Neave saw his expression and her grin widened. "Just don't set them off on any boats, and we'll be fine." She returned her gaze to Jame and Nalissa. "As I was saying: the mill should be empty by the time we get there. Two clockwork guards will be stationed inside the front door; we can't get to the mine shaft without sneaking in and getting rid of them first. That's your job."

They both nodded—Jame more confidently than Nalissa, dipped her chin stiffly.

Neave tore a piece of bread in two and chewed on the end. "The mill's not a complicated building to navigate. It's a giant square. The warden's office is on the north wall, here." She plucked a metal carabiner from the pile of gear and sat it on the table. "The doors to the mine shaft are on the east wall, and the guards will be stationed at the front door, to the south." She put a pair of binoculars and a firework down, respectively. "You two find a secondary way into the building, dispatch the guards, and let us into the front door. Winn's going to work her metal magic on the doors to the mine shaft, and—" Neave snapped her fingers. "The fun can really begin."

Jame scraped a piece of hair behind his ear, staring at Neave's makeshift map. "How tall is the building?"

"Five stories," Neave replied. "There's catwalks and partial floors up top, but in the center it's an open space, like a warehouse."

Jame bent over the map, thinking. Jack didn't have to see his face to know what he was considering; five stories and only partial floors meant there was an obvious weak point. Somewhere that would be less guarded than the front door.

Jack used his index finger to push the closest object—a flashlight—into the map. "There's a fire escape on the outside of the building," he said. "To the west."

This earned him a roguish grin. Jame rubbed his palms together. "Then that's where I think we should go." He half-turned to Nalissa, casting his eyes down to the table again. "Thoughts?"

Nalissa swallowed audibly, not looking up. "You mean we'll sneak in from the roof?"

"Good thing we have Thieves," Neave said, picking an invisible hair off the sleeve of her top. "Not much for climbing, myself."

Night came more quickly than Jack would have liked. He spent the evening watching Neave split their gear into six and flipping through his stolen copy of *Ancient Benemournian Rituals and Their Uses.* He'd skimmed through the opening chapters—*Origins of Ritual-Making, The Shute as Mystic Site, Keystones*—but the book hadn't told him anything he didn't know. The histories of ritual-making and keystones were a Treasure-hunter's expertise, and even regular folk knew the Shute had been considered a mystic place. There were enough forgotten ritual sites and sightings of strange creatures left over from centuries past.

Still, there had to have been a reason someone would hide this book behind a secret door in Fort Upper's library. There must have been *something* special inside it—something he couldn't learn anywhere else.

It was hard to read, however, while keeping one eye on the door to Little Space, waiting for the Head Inspector to come in. Jack didn't *want* to anticipate seeing Cameron, but the words on the page blurred all the same. Did Cameron regret bringing Jack on this expedition? Is that why someone had burned all the Adrudian in Jack's lantern, so that Jack and his false map could be *useful*?

Still, the sun leached from Little Space's windows and Cameron didn't arrive. When the time came, Jack returned his book to his jacket, next to *Gravel and Lode: Rocks and Gemstones of the Shute* and the flask of Adrudian Milk. He waved away Neave's offer of a weapons belt and returned to his room upstairs to put on his own. It was loose, hanging off his hips. Jack bore a new hole in the belt with the tip of his dagger, buckled it on, and left for their meeting place on the beach. He didn't bother looking in the mirror.

The air outside the tavern was spongy, so humid it left a sheen of moisture on the back of Jack's neck. The evening was new enough for the beach merchants to be selling the last of their wares, but old enough that the ferries had stopped running. The Adrudian lanterns lining the ferry dock had been shut, leaving a long strip of darkness reaching over the water.

Jack picked his way across the sand toward the dock, adjusting the buckles on the backpack Neave had given him. She had stored Jack's headlamp and other equipment in such a way that his movement was silent—a nice touch, he had to admit. A good Treasurehunter knew how to be quiet.

The shadows near the water were thick enough that Jack bumped into Nalissa, who jumped, startled. She was standing alone at the mouth of the ferry dock. Like Neave, she had changed into black for the expedition, her top hidden beneath what Jack guessed was a buttoned Casret Academy-issue blazer. She had pinned her brown, curled tresses back from her face, the length of her hair sweeping her collar. The trident she'd stolen was collapsed and slung over her back—incorrectly again.

Jack stepped onto the dock and leaned against the railing. Nalissa's eyes flicked toward him, then back over the dim sea. Her right hand was up at her neck, fist clenched around the keyhole pendant.

"You're early," Jack said, breaking the silence. He was early, too; their group wasn't supposed to meet for ten more minutes. He'd hoped for a few minutes with Cameron, who had the habit of being places he didn't need to be.

Nalissa swallowed, her jaw looking stiff and tight as stone. "I couldn't stay inside any longer." It was impossible to tell if she was nervous or excited. Her voice quaked a little. "Needed to get some air. To think."

Jack gestured to her hand clutching the lock. "And that helps you think?"

She glanced down at her fist, but didn't relinquish her hold on the pendant. Her wide, dark eyes grew distant. "It helps me ... hope, I guess."

Jack didn't much care for hoping, but he supposed he did it anyway. If he didn't, he wouldn't be here, headache sinking his body into the ground, elbows poking into the wood of the railing on this empty dock, a flask of Adrudian Milk in his pocket. He inhaled a lungful of salt-thick air.

"Your roommate." He imagined the corpse under the coverlet, a corner of fabric brushing the toe of his boot. That night seemed years ago. "She wasn't the one who grew up with that pendant. *You* did."

Nalissa's mouth pinched. Her gaze rested on Jack, then twitched away again. "Did Cameron tell you?"

Jack laughed despite himself. "No. I figured it out all on my own."

She raised her chin and said nothing, offering no explanation. Her outline looked so small against Ar's twinkling mountain that Jack felt an abrupt twinge of pity. Years in a Watch Academy had clearly dried her Thief's confidence. She couldn't even keep secrets. Her emotions skimmed over her face like mist over a glassy lake.

Bring her, and if you Drink, I'll show you.

"Lying has its merits." Jack bowed his head, grimacing as the back of his neck stretched. The sea frothed against the edge of the dock, staining the boards dark. "With you and that pendant, we have our best shot." He paused, then added, "But not if you can't get that trident off your back."

Nalissa dropped the pendant and wrapped a hand protectively around her shoulder. "What do you mean?"

"I mean," Jack said, "sling it properly. Like this." He opened his hand on the left side of his chest, sweeping his palm up over his shoulder.

Nalissa opened her mouth to argue, then seemed to decide it wouldn't be worth the breath. She brought the sling over her head, shifting her backpack. The trident slipped over her upper arm, but she fiddled with the sling's buckles until it fell into place. When she looked up, her expression was a question.

Jack nodded. "Didn't teach you much, did they? At that school."

She resumed squeezing the pendant in her fist, face

dropping into a frown. "They taught us how to fight with weapons, not carry them. The City Watch is supposed to teach us that."

Jack had the sudden image of Cameron teaching a room of Nalissas how to sling their weapons. It was almost comical how little the King cared about the efficacy of the Watch.

"Keep the lock close, but worry about your trident first," Jack said. The instruction came naturally, as if the woman in the mines' request had cemented in his mind overnight. *Bring her.* Keep her alive. "That pendant won't defend you from a clockwork that wants to rip out your arms."

Nalissa winced, but before she could reply, footsteps approached from across the beach. Four silhouettes detached themselves from the shadows: Jame, his backpack buckled across his chest; Cameron, tall and angular and draped in expensive gear; Winn, with her blue scarf and a brown leather tool belt wrapped around her waist; and Neave, who was grinning wickedly at each of them.

"I was wondering where you two were." Neave strode onto the dock behind Jack, sure-footed despite the darkness. Jack flattened his feet as the dock bobbed. "Any sign of the ferry? Knots should have been here by now."

Jack and Nalissa exchanged glances, as if each was hoping the other would reply. Finally, Jack cleared his throat. "No, no sign of him."

Cameron walked out onto the dock after Neave,

passing Jack in a waft of candle wax. His eyes slid over Jack as if he weren't there. Jack glowered at Cameron's back, watching him lift his binoculars and peer out over the sea. He thought he recognized the binoculars—bronze, shiny, the best of their kind. Cameron was wearing his old weapons belt, each buckle polished and shining like new. He looked so much like he had a year ago that Jack's ribs shrank.

"There," Cameron said, and the sound of a coughing engine rumbled out of the dark. A hulking, jumbled form materialized on the horizon. Jack didn't need binoculars to make out its shape. Knots' ferry resolved itself against the tossing waves, the Captain himself appearing on the bow as it approached. A little moonlight flashed as he smiled.

"Docking my boat in the dark," he yelled over to them as he pulled to a rocking stop at the head of the dock. "It's like you finally want this vessel at the bottom of the ocean, Neave."

"I'd like nothing better than to send it—and you—to a watery grave," Neave replied, jolly. She clasped her hand into Knots' and let him pull her aboard.

The rest of them followed, stepping to the edge of the dock and clambering onto the ferry. Jack earned another powerful clap on the back from the Captain—"Jack Fael, again! Looks like I'll be seeing more of you than I'd like," Knots said with a wink—but thankfully Jack's backpack absorbed it and kept him from careening off the side of the ship.

Winn was the last to climb aboard. She was so slight compared to Captain Knots that he practically lifted her up onto the deck. As he set her down, he took a good look at her face, eyes going wide.

"A Just." His booming voice had reduced to a whisper, the shabby folds of his Captain's coat seeming to puff in surprise.

"The only Just." Winn met his gaze, clearly expecting a challenge. She craned her neck to give the Captain a level stare, and Jack's fingertips tingled. Captain Knots had been Cameron's ally for years, but ferrying Winn Just was another matter. There was no telling how he might react to the Princess—he might be loyal to the Seven Thrones, but he also might get worked up about treason and end their expedition before they even left Ar's beach.

A quiet beat followed, during which Captain Knots and Winn peered at each other. Winn's springy coils of hair pulled back from her face and ruffled in the breeze. Out of the corner of his eye, Jack spied Neave's hand lifting toward her weapons belt—but finally the Captain broke their eye contact, having been outstared.

"Never thought I'd see you here, is all." He enveloped Winn's fingers in both his giant hands, hardly the bone-crushing handshake he usually gave. When he released her, he smacked the ferry's hull. "She looks like she's falling apart, but she'll keep you safe, Princess. My word."

A relieved murmur passed through their group. Knots retreated to the bridge, his barrel-wide shoulders disappearing through a low door. As the engine roared and the ferry pulled away from the beach, the six of them dispersed across the empty deck. Nalissa and Jame shuffled to opposite sides of the ship, sitting heavily on the metal benches. Neave rested against the railing, adjusting her backpack as Ar's mountain grew small behind them. Cameron drew Winn aside and they put their heads together, whispering.

Jack walked away from the others, fingers gliding over the cold metal railing. There was a nagging sensation in his middle, an unease that had forked from his usual restlessness. He leaned over the side of the ferry, gazing at the rolling waves being churned into foam by the boat's engine. On a clear day, he might be able to see his reflection cutting across the sea, rippling until it was a featureless, formless shimmer. Now, the ocean was a murky darkness. His arms itched and he dug a finger into his sleeve, dragging a nail across his skin.

For the hundredth time that day, Jack wished he had his notebook. His thoughts were trapped like insects on the inside of his skull. There was no writing for them to escape into, no blank page offering a respite from his own mind.

But a pen—he had a pen.

Jack reached into his jacket and retrieved his copy of *Ancient Benemournian Rituals and Their Uses*. Flipping to a random page, he pulled out a pen and wrote in the margin:

Bring the girl into the mines. Find the House of Matchsticks. Uncover the memory.

He paused, ink blotting the paper, then wrote:

Don't let him distract you.

Jack glanced across the deck, to where Cameron and Winn were talking, their outlines huddled close. The soft line of Winn's jaw shifted as she spoke. Cameron set a hand on her shoulder, listening, long fingers pressing into her sleeve.

The book closed with a *clap*. Jack turned and slid it into his jacket, shaking his head to clear the ringing from his ears. Before long, the great heap of shadows that was the mill would appear on the horizon. Then, he suspected, he would be able to think.

9

CLOCKWORK THIEVES

ISALINE

Find a way into the mill. Dispatch the guards. Let Neave, Winn, Cameron, and Jack through the front door.

Run away.

The last thought belonged to Isaline's nerves, a trailing mental fog that thickened as the mill approached. She perched on one of the ferry's metal benches, hugging her arms around her chest. Night had descended to its full weight and her stomach had started to churn, a cruel parody of the awe she felt last night, leaning over the edge of the ferry, watching Ar emerge under a twinkling sky. The mill appeared not as a sparkling mountain, but an angular, hulking shadow resting atop the sea. A hole in a void of blackness.

Captain Knots slowed the ferry to a stop and helped Isaline and the others off deck. They toed onto a ragged, slimy dock, lit with two Adrudian lanterns hanging over the water. A handful of bobbing rowboats lined each side.

"Don't like this place," Knots said as he released Isaline's hand. "Filled with spirits, this time of night."

That done, the Captain pulled the ferry straight back to sea and left them standing on the dock, shivering in the frigid air. The roar of the boat's engine faded into the murky horizon. He had promised to pick them up in three days. The stretch of hours between then and now seemed endless to Isaline, a hollow in time. Three days underground; three days during which she wouldn't see the sun. She counted her breaths as the six of them stole toward the Adrudian mill.

Darkness on the island was oppressive, blotting out the dock, the stony beach, even Isaline's feet as she steadied herself on the swaying wood. The mill itself was a ghostly silhouette ahead, its perimeter bathed dimly in scattered orange light. The only thing that kept Isaline moving forward was the feeling of her pendant tucked into the collar of her shirt—and the promise that if she followed this through, she would learn how it came to her.

Jame shuffled along the dock beside her with his arms crossed against the cold. His closeness made her chest ache. They hadn't looked at each other all day, and every time she wanted to speak to him, her voice dried and disappeared. Not talking about the kiss seemed impossible, but talking about it was somehow impossible, too. She was terrified the truth would slip from her mouth, ending the expedition before it began.

"Here we are," Neave whispered from the head of their procession. She unclipped her flashlight from her weapons belt and rolled her thumb over the dial, opening the bulb's slats and releasing a trisected beam of light.

The mill resolved into a huge, weathered brick box. Rows of filthy windows lined the outside, shining from within patches of spreading erosion on the walls. A warped, sliding metal door faced their party from the other end of a concrete square. The door was crumpled and discolored, but it looked impossibly heavy, as if cut out of the side of an airship hangar.

Cameron thumbed his own flashlight, a second fire-colored beam joining Neave's. He led them across the concrete square and up to the building, where they huddled in a circle. Isaline rested her palm in the center of a patch of crumbling brick. The mill didn't have the warmth of the Harper and Cup, or the authority of the buildings at Casret; it felt dead, empty.

"The clockwork guards are on the other side of that door," Winn said, her voice hushed. Her sharp, dark eyes reflected the orange light, turning into marbles. "Remember: they can't see you, but they'll sense you if you make noise or come close to them. Jame, Nalissa—we'll wait here. Good luck."

Isaline's blood quickened. She looked around. Was that it? The possibility of getting caught loomed large in

Isaline's mind. She trusted herself to be able to deal with the clockworks, but she'd never broken into a building before.

You're meant to be here, she reminded herself. Cameron's words from last night had become a prayer. *You can do this.*

Next to her, Jame eased out of the circle, his feet quiet as a breeze. He unclipped his flashlight and shone it around the corner of the building. His shadow stretched long and thin behind him. After a moment, he beckoned to Isaline and disappeared around the corner. Isaline took one last look at the rest of them before following, her heart thumping in her ears.

On the other side of the building, a fire escape snaked up the wall. Zigzagging stairs rose through the air like the iron vines of a creeping plant, casting barred shadows over the brick. Isaline brightened her flashlight. The bottom platform hung eight feet off the ground, and the rest was *high*. At the top, her flashlight's beam diffused into the canopy of the sky, dimly illuminating a battered eaves' edge. She imagined Nalissa dancing along the roof, saying, *Turn upside down. Gives you a new perspective.*

On those nights, Nalissa had left Isaline shivering in the middle of the roof, too afraid to approach the sides. Now, there was no choice but to climb, suspended in the air on a thin iron grille. Her heart galloped. She should have told someone about her fear of heights—but who? Would Nalissa have been afraid?

Jame lingered beneath the fire escape. He glanced at her, his attention settling heavily on her awareness. Isaline grip tightened on the flashlight. An intuition had grown in her overnight, a sense that detected the suggestion of his gaze, the hint of his breaths, his proximity to her. Being alone with him now gave her a nervous excitement that nearly eclipsed her fear of climbing.

"Here's the fire escape," Jame said, as if Isaline hadn't been staring at it for half a minute. His voice was tentative. Not nervous about the climb, but about talking to her. "Are you ready?"

No.

"Yes," Isaline said.

"Give me a boost."

Steeling herself, Isaline braced her back against the wall and laced her fingers. Jame stepped onto her hands. His weight made her muscles smart. Her arms were still recovering from her Weapons Portion—injuries that had happened a lifetime ago, to another Isaline. She marveled at how different she could feel inside the same body, bearing old bruises.

You were right, Nalissa, she thought as Jame caught hold of the fire escape and pulled himself onto its platform. *I should have been more careful.*

"Easy as that." Jame's voice fell from above her.

"Sure," was all Isaline could think of to say. She shook the tension from her hands, then jumped and caught his extended arm. His fingers closed around her wrist, pulled, and she flopped onto the fire escape. The freezing metal bit into her knees as she got unsteadily to her feet.

Don't look down.

The ground seemed too far to be only eight feet away. Jame released her arm, the warmth of his touch leaving an impression through her sleeve. They stood in silence for a moment before he turned and started up the stairs, taking them two at a time.

Unspoken words dissolved on Isaline's tongue. She didn't know what she wanted to say to him, but the pockets of time in which to say it were shrinking.

"Get it together," she muttered to herself, following Jame up the steps. She fixed her eyes on the railing to keep from looking at the ground.

The brick wall grew more and more weathered as she scaled the fire escape, as if the mill were breaking apart from the top down. Years of battering rain and sea wind had blanketed the iron platforms in rust. The grille was rickety beneath Isaline's feet. *Great.* The fire escape was unstable. She tried to ignore the deep, creaking whines of the iron as she joined Jame at the top.

Jame tipped his head over the railing, peering at the ground below. "Cold up here," he said, pulling his coat closer around him.

Isaline hadn't noticed the temperature. She was too busy gripping the railing, fingers rigid. Now that they were on the top platform, just beneath the lip of the roof, the empty space below threatened to lock her legs. She held her breath, rocking side to side. Sea crashed against shore somewhere below them. *Far* below them.

"Do you think they ever meant for anyone to actually use this thing?" Jame sent his flashlight over their feet, examining the worn metal. Isaline couldn't help it; her eyes moved down of their own accord. The space below them seemed to stretch, expanding until the ground was small enough to hide behind the flat of her hand.

"It's not built very well," Jame continued, rubbing a thumb along the metal, "or maintained at all. It looks a hundred years old."

"S-stop talking," Isaline said. She barely squeaked the words out of her lungs.

Jame looked at her fully now, eyebrows coming together. "What's wrong?"

"I don't like ... I *really* don't like—" Isaline's sentence died as the platform let out a long groan. "Oh, no."

The grille shuddered, sending ripples through her knees. The supports were weak—even weaker than she'd thought—and the whole fire escape was straining under their weight. Isaline's reflexes took control of her legs. She backed away from the railing, but just that movement was enough to make the fire escape groan again. The platform shook and swayed, pulling against the bolts embedded in the crumbling brick wall.

"That's not good," Jame said under his breath.

"You think?" Isaline replied, but her voice was

drowned out by another whine. The sound sent a shiver all the way to her stomach.

Jame hovered at her side, clearly unsure where to move. *If* to move. Somewhere beneath them, a bar crunched. The platform tilted a few inches, throwing Isaline's balance to the left. She bent her knees, sliding down to a crouch against the wall, little moans escaping her mouth. The trident bit into her shoulder.

"This way!"

Jame's voice, and his movement to her side, but Isaline could hardly see him. Fear had turned her vision white. She squeezed her eyes shut, imagining the stomach-dropping terror of plummeting five stories. The crash of metal against concrete, the agony of her bones smashing.

Another support beneath them snapped. The platform dipped, forcing her to curl into a ball to stay upright.

It's going to fall. It's going to fall, it's going to fall, it's going to fall.

The platform trembled, then went still.

Isaline counted three seconds. Five. She cracked an eye open. The fire escape was still upright, bolted to the side of the building. A support on the platform below had broken, destabilizing the top of the structure, but that was all. Isaline was still alive, and Jame ...

"Jame?" Isaline blinked, and blinked again. Jame didn't appear—the fire escape was empty. "Where are you?"

"Check your hand."

His voice came from above her. She lifted her gaze, and there was her hand, clutching Jame's arm so tightly it was numb. Beyond it was the rest of him; he had hauled himself onto the roof and was lying casually across the eave's edge, dangling one arm for Isaline to grip with all her strength.

"You know," he said, his grin partially hidden behind his forearm, "if you're on a falling fire escape, it's probably best to get off."

Relief flooded through her, followed by a spreading, hot flush. She peeled her fingers from Jame's sleeve.

"Well, it didn't fall, did it?" Isaline eased to her feet, wincing as the fire escape let out another, smaller groan. "Get me off this thing."

Jame took her hand and helped her over the edge. The mill's roof was similar to her dormitory's: a flat expanse of deteriorating concrete with a roof access at the far end. Isaline rushed into the middle of the roof and sank to her hands and knees, breathing hard.

A light chuckle came from behind her as Jame stood from the roof's edge.

"Heights, is that it?" He strolled over to her, one hand stuck in his pocket. "You really don't like heights."

Isaline rocked back to sit on her heels, pressing a hand over her chest. Her heart was pounding, leaving her limbs wobbly. "Really, *really* don't."

"Can't find firewood, can't build a fire, can't stand heights ..." Jame counted out each on his fingers.

"I'm glad you think this is funny," Isaline said, glaring at him, but his amused expression gave her another flood of relief. One smile was better than the cold sheet of glass that had been stretched between them all day. One smile was a start.

"Good thing you're an excellent fighter. I've seen that much." He paused, then asked, "Anything else I should know about you?"

"No." She tipped her head back to stare at the sky. There were no stars ahead, no moon. Clouds reached from horizon to horizon. "Nothing at all."

JAME MADE short work of the lock on the roof access enclosure. As Isaline readjusted the trident's sling, he passed his palm over the lock and it rattled open, as if by magic.

"Not very secure, is it?" Isaline murmured, peering into the slice of dark behind the door.

"Doesn't have to be," Jame replied. He returned a thin, bronze instrument to his sleeve—some kind of unlocking tool—and pressed his ear to the door jamb, listening. "Only someone with a death wish would break into a building filled with clockworks in the middle of the night."

She shot him a quizzical expression.

"Someone with a death wish, or ..." He thumbed his

flashlight closed and cheerfully pushed the door open. "Or whoever *we* are."

Isaline closed her own flashlight, gritting her teeth as night swept in. "Careful people?"

"Sure." Jame toed his way into the roof access enclosure. "Careful."

They felt their way down a set of stairs, around a sharp turn, and finally through a heavy door that opened onto the top floor of the mill. As Isaline stepped inside, a thick, chalky odor made her stop short. Her nostrils spasmed, sending a warning to her gag reflex. The air was thick with Adrudian, the smell even more powerful than at Upper Train Station.

Jame pinched the tip of his nose. "I found a decaying possum in a chimney stack once," he whispered. "This is worse."

Isaline blinked water from her eyes and the interior of the mill came into focus. She and Jame were standing at the edge of a metal balcony overlooking the mill's interior. The cavernous room was dark, save for the sprinkled amber glow of Adrudian ore, piled up under tarps or spilling out of wheelbarrows. Catwalks stretched between the partial floors ringing the inside of the building, supporting pulleys and piles of equipment. Below them, shadows crept along the mill's massive, thorny forest of iron machines.

She stared, too astounded to be afraid of the height. So much machinery in one place—she couldn't imagine the commotion when it was all running at once, managed by hundreds of mill workers. Now, when the mill was closed, it was so silent her own breaths seemed deafening.

Jame unclipped his binoculars and brought them to his face. "There," he said, pointing straight ahead.

He passed the binoculars to Isaline, and she followed his gaze to the east wall, where a set of bronze double doors glinted in the darkness. At the base of the door, the telltale marks of passing wheelbarrows were just visible. This was the door to the mine shaft. Next to it, a tiny control box protruded from the wall—the mechanism Winn was going to use to admit them onto the lift.

"And there," Jame continued. He pressed his fingers briefly over hers, turning her toward the south wall.

She knew what she was going to find, but still Isaline's stomach kicked. The clockwork guards were standing motionless by the warped front door. Each was tall and thin, with a blank wooden lump as a face. Patches of orange the size of dinner plates shone out of their bellies.

The last time she had fought a clockwork, she'd been confident. Her nerves quiet as midnight. She'd fought five different sparring clockworks in her time at Casret Academy. If she could only access that other Isaline, the Isaline that existed before, she could do this.

You can do this.

"Let's go," Jame said.

They tiptoed down the stairs, taking the grated panels more slowly than they had the fire escape. The steps skirted the mill's floors, steepening as they turned onto the wall ahead. Jame kept close to the railing with his shoulders held loosely back. Isaline mimicked his posture, too anxious to dare another look over the side.

At the edge of the north wall, they passed a massive panel spread with hundreds of buttons. Jame paused midstride and stared at it. He glanced over his shoulder at Isaline.

"Do you think it controls the machines on the floor?" he whispered. "Or turns on the power, maybe?"

She had no clue. There had never been technology like this at the academy. But Jame was likely right: painted letters above one giant, orange switch read *Power*. The toggle had been flicked to *On*.

They continued down the stairs, leaving the panel behind. The dark grew dense and the mill's iron spires rose to meet them. Jame slowed his pace near the third floor; they were coming up to the edge of a large, faintly glowing window. The warden's office. Light leaked through the glass, casting a misshapen rectangle on the stairs.

Isaline backed against the wall as Jame peeked through the window. He moved so quickly her eyes almost didn't catch it; one moment, the hair at the top of his head was illuminated, then it flicked into shadows.

"Empty," he whispered to her. "The warden left her lamp open."

He moved aside so Isaline could take her own look

through the window. The office was closet-sized, with two metal-backed chairs sitting beside a wooden desk piled high with papers. On the floor, a small pool of whiskey had dried into a sticky round next to an overturned, empty bottle. An Adrudian lamp hung from the ceiling, slats wide open.

Isaline bit her lip as Jame led her down the rest of the stairs. Why would the warden leave her lamp open? To deter Thieves? But Jame was right: No one would try to break into the mill. It was too dangerous. Maybe the warden had simply forgotten to close it, after drinking a bottle of whiskey and tottering out to the ferry.

A moment later, Isaline took her first steps onto the concrete floor of the mill. Countless machines soared above them, draping the narrow aisles in shadows. Isaline wiggled her toes in her boots. The floor was flush against her feet. Firm. *Solid.* Even though she had just sneaked into a building armed by clockwork guards, her legs trembled with relief. She crept after Jame into the small space between an iron furnace and a pile of covered Adrudian.

We made it.

They had climbed and descended five stories in the space of ten minutes. Letting out a long breath, Isaline slumped against the furnace and rubbed a hand over her face.

"Don't get too comfortable," Jame whispered, brushing a smear of soot off his sleeve. His rings sparkled in the thin light seeping from beneath the covered Adrudian. "There's still clockworks to fight."

"The clockworks are the easy part, though, compared to that." Isaline gestured to the stairway winding up to the roof. Jame's expression softened as she passed a hand over her moist forehead. "I'd fight ten clockworks before climbing that fire escape again."

"*Ten*?" He adjusted the straps on his backpack, giving her a sly smile. "Maybe we should scale a ten-story building next time, then, to even things out. Ten stories is easy."

The thought of hanging more than a hundred feet off the ground made the pressure inside Isaline's head pulse. She waved Jame's suggestion away. "No thanks. I'll have to pass."

"What happens next time, then?"

Isaline considered this, wondering what she would have said if Nalissa had broached the same question. Finally, she said, "We'll have to knock the building down."

"Knock it down?" Jame let out an abrupt laugh, stifling the sound with the back of his hand. "Ten stories?"

"I thought you said it was easy."

He looked so startled that a laugh pulled from Isaline's own mouth, and another from his. They spent a few moments chuckling silently into their palms, darkness spilling into either side of their resting spot. The laughter eased a tension in Isaline's chest, and when she lowered her hand, the fog of her nerves had cleared, just a bit.

"Fine, you're right," Jame said when he had collected himself. "Maybe climbing the fire escape wasn't the best plan. But neither is jumping a couple of clockwork guards."

Isaline agreed. Regardless, she was feeling more confident than she had all evening. "We should probably get on it, then."

Minding the staff of her trident, she sidled past Jame and peeked around the corner of the Adrudian pile. Beyond it was an empty aisle leading through rows of machines. If Isaline had her bearings, the aisle would lead them to the south wall, toward the clockworks and the rest of their team, crouched behind the front door.

"This way." She beckoned to him, then tiptoed into the darkness.

Jame whistled a few tuneless notes under his breath and followed.

The aisle was confined and difficult to navigate, their path taking bend after bend to skirt worn conveyor belts, wide-mouthed vats, and still more piles of Adrudian. Stocky wheelbarrows leaned heavily against railings, deactivated clockwork pickaxers slumped over their handles like sleepers. The snicked points of pickaxes extended seamlessly from the clockworks' arms. Limbs immobile, bellies unlit, they resembled giant, abandoned puppets.

A tingle erupted on the back of Isaline's neck. She counted nine pickaxers, and those were only the ones in sight. They were bigger and bulkier than the clockwork guards, built for hacking stone deep below the earth. She reached back and ran her fingers along her trident. The pickaxers wouldn't wake unless someone said their activation phrase, but the sight of so many jumbled bodies chilled her.

Somewhere behind her, Jame's feet were quiet as a murmur. She could only be sure of his presence by his whistling, still tuneless and hushed. Isaline was grateful for the sound. Without it, the silence would have been suffocating, the mill transformed into a clockwork graveyard.

As they neared the front door, Jame's fingers whispered on her palm.

"I think the guards are on the other side of this machine," he said in her ear. A giant machine that resembled a waterwheel loomed to their left, attached to an immense vat brimming with uncooked Adrudian. "You should stop whistling."

The words took a moment to register. Isaline halted, extending a hand to keep them from colliding. "I thought *you* were whistling."

"I'm not."

His words disappeared into the dark. Isaline went still.

The breathy whistle floated through the air again. This time, it clearly wasn't coming from Jame, who was standing close enough for the warmth of his shoulder to touch hers. The sound came from behind them, from the mill's front door. From the clockworks.

Ice worked its way into Isaline's veins.

There's someone else here.

Before the thought had time to sink in, Jame locked his fingers onto Isaline's hand. He pulled her into the shadows and ducked into the cramped space beneath the wheel machine. Isaline slid next to him, smearing grime and soot on the calves of her trousers.

The hiding space afforded them a narrow view of the mill's front door. Isaline peered around Jame's knees, the tip of her nose brushing his legs. Only three steps away, the clockwork guards stood unmoving on either side of the door. Their feet were flat, hoof-like, their long limbs resembling the knobbed and twisted joints of marionettes. Short swords protruded from each handless arm, just long enough for the sharp points to be visible resting by their ankles.

And there, standing between the guards, was a squat, yellow-haired woman. She was whistling as she fiddled with a bronze padlock hanging from the mill's front door. Isaline recognized what she thought were mill worker's clothes, complete with a grubby pair of goggles strapped around the back of the woman's head. The smell of whiskey enveloped her like a shroud.

The mill warden.

She was still here. She had stayed the night. The rest of Isaline and Jame's team were on the other side of that door, separated by only a slab of metal.

Watching the warden tug on the padlock, testing its

strength, a storm of images broke into Isaline's mind. She imagined the warden pressing her face to the narrow opening of their hiding spot; dragging Isaline out by the feet, bringing her face-to-face with the clockwork guards; ordering the guards to stab Jame with the point of a sword.

Jame wrapped his hand around her twitching fingers, squeezing. He leaned close to her ear.

"Look. She's leaving."

They held their breath, watching as the warden slid a carved bronze key out of the padlock. She attached it noisily to an iron ring, then dropped the whole thing in the pocket of her coat. Still whistling, she strolled away in the direction of her office. Isaline and Jame sat frozen, curled against each other in the tiny space. The clomps of her boots faded into the distance.

"That's a Thieflock," Jame whispered, words barely audible. "We can't open it without that key. Not quietly, at least."

Isaline had no idea what a Thieflock was, but she nodded.

"New plan, then." Jame scanned the darkness on either side of their hiding place, staring down the end of his pointed nose. "I'll go pick the warden's pocket. Lock her in her office, maybe. You deal with the clockworks."

For a moment, Isaline simply stared at him. Then she said, "Both of them?"

"Both of them." To her amazement, he winked at her. "It's hardly ten."

She had the urge to kick him, but it wasn't as if she could refuse. With the warden here, they had to act fast.

Jame squeezed her hand again, and she nodded. She crawled out of the hiding space, Jame following close behind, and they struggled silently to their feet. Isaline gulped and rubbed her dirty hands on the legs of her pants. Her palms had broken into a sweat.

"Jame, wait." She tugged on his coat to catch his attention before he slunk back down the aisle. "The warden locked the front door with a Thieflock. Does that mean—"

"She was expecting us?" Jame's eyes flashed, with worry or excitement Isaline couldn't tell. His breath puffed against her cheek. "I don't know, but I thought of it, too. Thieflocks are expensive—she's up to something. Be careful."

"You, too."

He hesitated, then inclined his head and gave her a secretive smile. "Just so we're clear," he said, "I'd do it again. The beach. If you wanted to."

At first, Isaline wasn't sure what he meant, but then a warmth spread into her cheeks. "I know."

"Good."

He sneaked back the way they had come, vanishing into the forest of machines.

Alone in the dark, Isaline sneaked around the giant vat of unprocessed Adrudian. She cast a look over her shoulder toward the north side of the mill. The warden's office window sat high enough on the wall for her to have a clear view inside. The room was empty, for now. Orange light shone through the window, making a strange, rectangular sun.

Isaline chewed on her thoughts, turning up strategies for fighting the clockworks. She couldn't deactivate them —she didn't have their deactivation phrase—so there was no choice but to try to destroy them.

Her eyes swept her immediate area. An assortment of angular machines was packed closely around her, providing plenty of hiding places but not much room to move. The trident was too long to be of much use in these thin slices of space. She silently patted the floor with her boot. The floor was cracked and uneven, too. Dangerous to maneuver.

Ruling out the mill's floorspace, Isaline lifted onto the tips of her toes, trying to glimpse the edge of the vat. It was taller than she—maybe ten feet. Beyond the vat's edge, she could just see the top of a pile of Adrudian heaped inside. The rocks were too uncooked to be emitting much light.

She slunk in the shadows until she found something promising around the side of the vat: a small set of stairs leading up to an iron platform skirting the edge of the vat.

Up there, maybe she could find the space to fight. Maybe.

She gingerly ascended the steps, keeping an eye on the north wall. The warden's tangle of yellow hair had appeared, ascending the metal staircase toward the office window. Isaline hoped the spread of machines between them would be enough to hide her from sight.

She crossed the iron platform as quietly as possible. To her right, the huge vat lay open, its pile of dimly glowing Adrudian level with her ankles. End to end, the vat was the size of a small swimming pool. The horrible smell coming from it was almost tangible. She slipped a hand over her mouth to keep from gagging.

The wheel machine hulked ahead, its enormous iron spokes sitting close to the platform's end. Like the vat, the wheel was larger than she had thought. Isaline craned to gaze at its apex, four times her height or more. There were concave scoops around its circumference, resembling the blades of shovels. The bottom half of the wheel plunged into the vat, buried beneath rocks of Adrudian. She guessed the wheel churned the Adrudian during the day.

Isaline had nearly come up to the end of the platform when something scampered behind her.

She whirled, her hand shooting reflexively to the trident. The space behind her appeared empty, wrapped in greasy orange light.

"Jame?" she whispered, glancing to the north wall. The warden was inside her office now, shuffling through papers. Jame was there, too, crouched beneath the window, no doubt preparing to steal her keys.

Isaline's heart rose into her throat. If Jame hadn't made the sound—then the clockworks? She peered through the bars of the wheel machine, but the heads of both clockworks were still there, immobile.

Another scamper teased Isaline's ear, closer now. Coming from somewhere to her left. The *pat-pat-pat* of little feet on metal.

This time, she turned slowly, fingers resting on the trident's edge. Two beady, blood-red eyes stared at her from the platform's railing, only a few steps away. Isaline peered into the dim and saw a brush of wiry whiskers.

A black rat.

It was perched on the top bar of the railing, flashing its long, gleaming teeth. Isaline relaxed her hands. Just a few days ago, she'd been so surprised by a squirrel in Casret's training area that she'd fallen on her backside. Maybe she'd grown braver in the time since her Weapons Portion after all.

The rat chewed and tilted its head, watching her with its fire-point eyes. Something poked out of the sides of its mouth: a clump of flaxen hair, being munched into tiny pieces. Isaline recognized the warden's blonde and let out an involuntary breath. How had this rat gotten a chunk of the mill warden's hair?

As she peered closer, the rat dropped off the railing and scurried toward her feet, its movement too fast to follow in the dim light. Isaline took a step backward, startled. The rat paused and looked up at her, its eyes cunning and hungry. Patches of fur were scrubbed from its skin, and its teeth were sharp and yellow-gray-black. Not a pet, or at least not a pet that got any grooming.

"Go away," Isaline whispered at it.

The rat made a little movement, like it was contemplating lunging at her feet. She took another step backward and the rat clicked its teeth at her, legs gathering beneath its body. A knot formed in Isaline's stomach. The clockworks were just on the other side of the wheel machine. If she had to bat this rat away, they would hear, and her advantage would be thrown.

She swept the side of her foot to shoo the rat, but it just stared at her. It made a half-grab for her boot, teeth flashing.

"No ..." Isaline backed farther still. The end of the platform was coming up behind her. She waved one hand. "Stop it, get away."

But her gestures only emboldened it. In a flash of black fur and pinkish skin, the rat leaped onto her right foot and sank its top teeth into the toe of her boot.

Isaline twisted, swallowing the yelp that threatened to burst from her mouth. She kicked her leg. Nalissa's boots were made of thick leather, too thick for the rat's teeth to pierce her skin, but it clamped itself onto her foot and wouldn't budge.

"No, hey! No!" Isaline couldn't tell if she was whispering or merely mouthing the words. She briefly envisioned attacking the rat with the prongs of the trident, but she didn't know if she could bring herself to kill it—and she couldn't stab it without sticking her foot in the process.

Isaline kicked out again. She came up against the end of the platform. Something big and rectangular pressed into her backpack. It wasn't the railing she'd expected; the surface of it *gave.* Pushed inward with a tiny, barely audible *click.*

A moment's silence, then an ear-bursting roar split the air behind her. Isaline's bones jolted, and she stumbled forward, reversing direction. She was only vaguely aware of the rat releasing her foot. It went running down the side of the platform, a black blur.

Shock weakened Isaline's legs, and she fell to her hands and knees. The air hissed out of her lungs—the loudest sound she'd made since climbing the fire escape. The sound was swallowed beneath the thundering noise that continued to rend the silence.

An earthquake, her mind offered. But it wasn't an earthquake. The platform beneath her was vibrating with a regular, gut-shaking rumble. The heap of Adrudian inside the vat sucked in on itself, then rose again. A churning wave.

All at once, Isaline understood. She flipped over, digging the heels of her hands into the trembling iron platform.

The wheel machine had come to life. It's great iron bulk turned in place, enormous scoops plunging and rising through the vat of Adrudian. To her left, a vast plain of orange rocks turned, roiled, and tumbled with the deafening sound of heaving gravel.

At the end of the platform, directly ahead of Isaline, was a control box. The shiny, red top button was smudged where the pockets of Isaline's dirty backpack had pressed it.

Jame.

Isaline twisted again and lifted her gaze to the north wall. Both Jame and the mill warden had frozen inside the office, staring with twin expressions of alarm through the window. Jame's arm was stretched out and grasping the ring of keys at the warden's belt. Even from this distance, Isaline thought she could see his forearm trembling.

Nearest to Isaline, by the door, the clockworks lifted their heads.

Isaline couldn't remember standing, but suddenly she was on her feet. Her mind registered the scene through the window on the north wall—the mill warden had spotted Jame at her elbow and pushed him, her lumpy face turning into a snarl—but the clockwork guards were a more immediate terror. The noise from the wheel machine had regulated into a loud, consistent rumble. Beneath it were the heavy thuds of clockwork feet coming toward her.

She checked the straps of her backpack, tightened the

buckles, and unslung her trident. The staff eased effortlessly from her shoulder, falling into her shaking hands. *Thank you, Jack.*

Hoping against hope that Jame was all right, Isaline pushed the button on the trident's staff, and it extended, three silver points clicking into place. She scanned the floor beyond the turning wheel machine. Between its rotating spokes, a view of the mill's front door was empty. As she had suspected, the clockworks had slid into motion and were approaching her, their steps smooth and mechanical.

One glossy, wooden head bobbed around the side of the Adrudian vat, cutting a straight course to the steps up the platform. The second clockwork had come the other way, making to hoist itself up onto the platform behind her.

They're surrounding me.

Isaline swallowed her panic and made the split-second decision to deal with the closest clockwork first. She spun on the spot and bent her knees, lifting the trident. The clockwork clambered onto the end of the platform, swung its knobby limbs over the railing, and thudded flat-footed only steps from where Isaline stood. Her legs absorbed the ripple of impact through the platform, ankles shuddering as the clockwork stretched to its full height, its blank no-face towering over her.

"Oh, stars," she said, or thought she said, before the

clockwork hefted its swords and brought both of them down towards her head.

She flung herself to the side, colliding with the railing and dodging the blow by a hair's width. The clockwork's swords crashed into the platform. The iron grille quaked. Not stopping to think, Isaline pushed herself from the railing and thrust the trident toward the clockwork's glowing belly. Her aim was true, but the clockwork was too fast: it pivoted, and her trident barely nicked its torso.

Out of the corner of her eye, Isaline noted the second clockwork's position: it hadn't reached the platform's steps yet. She had a few seconds, maybe less, to fight this first one before being attacked by the second.

The clockwork lunged at her with its sword-arms outstretched. Isaline parried and countered, and the metal of their weapons met with a *clang*. Her mind whirled as she fought it, trying to strategize. How was she going to destroy it?

Behind the clockwork's towering frame, the wheel machine rotated in a smooth, roaring *whoosh*. She took a millisecond to consider the thick iron scoops soaring up, around, and plunging into the vat of Adrudian.

She had an idea.

Time to improvise.

The clockwork rushed her, its swords flashing. Instead of bringing the trident up in defense, she evaded its arms and maneuvered to the side farthest from the Adrudian vat. Crying out, she thrust the prongs of the trident between the clockwork's feet. It tried to take a step but faltered, its balance upset.

Isaline was ready. She rammed her shoulder into the clockwork's wooden side, putting all the power she had into the push.

The clockwork tried to slash upward, but it missed and stumbled. Its feet lumbered around the trident. She'd hoped its weight and height would work against it—and she was beautifully, miraculously *right*.

Isaline stepped back as the clockwork dropped, teetering like a felled tree, and pitched over the railing, landing backward inside the Adrudian vat. Rocks of Adrudian rolled over its body, burying its legs up to the knees, then the waist. Adrudian was light, for a rock—but the ore was churning and slippery. The clockwork struggled. It couldn't unearth itself.

She had time to think only one word: *yes*. Then her intuition twanged, and she ducked. An iron sword passed where her head had been. She grasped the trident and rolled to the side, putting a paltry distance between herself and the second clockwork that had come up behind her.

The clockwork swung down with both its swords and Isaline raised the trident to block them. Steel clashed against iron, but the trident managed to meet the swords with enough force to stop them slicing her in half. Her heart sent a plea to her elbows, begging them not to give out as the clockwork doubled its weight against her.

"Nalissa!" It was Jame's voice. He had come rushing

between the vat and the huge container on its other side. She glanced at the edge of the vat and saw his hand streaking by, held high over his head, dangling a ring of keys from his thumb. He had somehow wrestled them from the warden.

The clockwork in front of her shifted—Isaline was crouched on the platform beneath it, holding its weapons at bay with only the staff of the trident—and *pushed.* Isaline's lower back screamed.

"*Open the door,*" she shouted to Jame. She released the tension in her arms, turned, and rocked to the right. Without her opposing force, the clockwork's blades shot down and buried themselves in the iron grille.

Her stomach flipped. If she had tried to hold out longer, that could have been her arm. Or her neck.

Jame's hand disappeared below the lip of the vat, heading in the direction of the door. "Keep fighting it! Then you can shut off the power upstairs!"

The clockwork wedged its arms out of the platform. Isaline blinked sweat out of her eyes.

"Thanks for the advice," she said under her breath.

She blocked another jab from the swords, and another. The clockwork was good at anticipating where she was going to move—if she feinted, it struck out with its sword and forced her to throw out the spear in defense. She tried to trip it like she had the other, but it just sidestepped the trident, as if it had learned from the mistakes of its fallen partner, now buried somewhere beneath the rolling Adrudian.

Isaline's arms burned. The clockwork had her backed up against the wheel machine, and her muscles were tiring. She wasn't sure she could hold out long enough for Jame to let the others in.

"Jame," she tried to say, but her voice was trapped behind her ragged breaths. The metallic jingling continued. He was unaware she needed his help—but how *could* he help? He had no weapons that would stand a chance against this clockwork guard.

No help. No options.

Options.

There was one other. The thought of it passed into her mind without proper examination. Nalissa would have laughed if she were here, an uproarious cackle that echoed in Isaline's ears louder than the thundering wheel machine.

That's ridiculous, Nalissa's voice intoned. *You'll get killed. Maimed, certainly.*

But as the clockwork's swords hit the grille again, shaking the platform so violently it was in danger of tipping over, Isaline realized she didn't have a choice. She needed more power than she had.

The clockwork wrenched its swords from the platform, taking spare seconds to roll its shoulders. Ignoring Nalissa's voice in her head, Isaline shuffled backward until the pockets of her backpack grazed the wheel machine's control box. She skirted it, stepping to the left, and pressed flush against the low railing at the end of the platform instead.

Isaline took a deep breath and held it. She was going against all of her training. Against every instinct she had.

She pressed the trident's middle grip, collapsing it. She flung it over the railing, along with her backpack. They clattered to the concrete floor.

Behind her, a breath away, the wheel machine rotated and thundered. Isaline sensed the thick metal bars passing smoothly inside the machine's stationary frame, scarcely an inch from her back. Hot, Adrudian-scented air belched over her shoulder, issuing from the wheel's gnashing metal mouths. She was too close to it. Any closer and she would be pulled inside. The bars would rend her.

I'm going to die, Isaline thought.

She shouted to the clockwork, "Come and get me!"

As if obeying her command, the clockwork raised its swords and attacked. Its footsteps rattled Isaline's teeth in her head. Dread descended upon her. The surrounding mill vanished, dimming until only she existed. Isaline, the clockwork, and the wheel.

The wheel.

She hurled herself over the railing and onto the side of the machine.

Her fingers scrabbled at a passing spoke, missed, then found purchase on one of the enormous scoops. The tendons in her shoulders jerked as she was yanked into the air. She found a foothold—an iron bar—and clung to the scoop with all the strength she had left. The floor and the platform dropped away. Her stomach plunged. She was carried high—*too high, too high*—up the side of the wheel.

"Just hold on," she heard herself saying. She pressed her face between her forearms. "Hold on, hold on, hold on ..."

The wheel carried her on a near-vertical ascent through the air, and then she was coming to the top. Gravity began to shift, tossing her insides. Jame came into view on the ground below. He was hunched over the Thieflock, trying key after key. His figure was so minute Isaline's eyes unfocused. She couldn't bear to see how far up she was. She couldn't ...

The machine jolted. A metallic, grinding whine pierced her ears. Isaline's vision lurched as the wheel came to an abrupt halt. Her center of gravity was flung forward, but she tightened her grip on the scoop, turning every muscle she had into rock.

She was at the top of the wheel. But it had stopped—why had it stopped?

The wheel's engine coughed. Its consistent roar had risen to an ear-grinding mechanical howl. Isaline clutched the scoop and peeked over the side of the machine, down to the platform. Smoke tickled her eyes.

Far below, the clockwork's legs kicked, half over the railing. The rest of it had fallen inside the wheel machine.

Her plan had *worked*. It tried to get up, but a spoke was pressing on its back.

The machine rumbled. Trembled. Rumbled again. Smoke billowed from some unknowable engine. Isaline squeezed her stinging eyes shut. Her pendant pressed into the hollow of her throat.

Please shut down. Just shut down, so I can climb down and be done with this.

Seconds later, with a sound like a tree splitting, the clockwork's body crunched in half.

Adrudian Milk sprayed the platform. Wooden legs fell to the chopped-up grille, kicking and thrashing wildly. Isaline took an instant to register her victory—*I did it!*—before the wheel machine hurtled forward with an explosion of built-up tension.

The world rushed by in a blur, the wheel's apex coming and going.

Isaline held her breath and flew.

10

STARMAP

JACK

An ear-shaking rumble reverberated through the mill's front door, near where Jack, Neave, Winn, and Cameron were waiting. To Jack, the noise was both strange and familiar, a mechanical scream driving through the silent island. He gritted his teeth. Nalissa and Jame were in trouble. If they weren't, they were being careless. Jack wasn't sure which was worse.

He stood, stretched his stiff legs, and leaned backward against the mill's patchy wall. The rocky shoreline of the island stretched before him, barely visible in the dark of night. Only twenty minutes had passed since Nalissa and Jame had vanished around the corner, but Jack's feet were restless.

"Permission to break down the door?" Neave pressed

her ear to the dimpled metal, wincing as it vibrated against her head. "Whatever's running inside, it's loud."

"Not yet," Winn said. She was standing a short distance away, lighting what seemed to be an entire book of matches one-by-one. Pinpoints of light flared, illuminating the white of Winn's teeth before hissing out. "We don't want to break something we can't repair, and it's only been a minute."

"A minute too long," Jack muttered. He pressed his fingers into his cheeks. The bridge of his nose ached, turning his still-fading hangover into a ball of cotton inside his skull.

Cameron was the only member of their party who seemed relaxed. He passed a steady hand through his hair. "Nalissa and Jame are fine," he said. "I bet they turned on a machine to distract the clockwork guards."

Jack looked at him askance. "They shouldn't have turned on a machine at all."

"Sure, but ..." Cameron picked at a thread on his sleeve. "Give them some time."

Scowling, Jack dug the toe of his boot into the dusty concrete. If it had been *his* expedition—just his, like every expedition had been before—he would have been in the mines by now. The stress of making an expedition alone was nothing compared to this intolerable waiting. His insides buzzed.

Minutes later—or hours; Jack lost count—a jingling sound segmented the mechanical rumble. The four of them stared at the door. Someone was trying keys on the other side.

"There we go." With a look of relief, Winn deposited the book of matches into her toolbelt. "Sounds like they're okay."

"Told you," Cameron said with a grin. He brushed the legs of his pants, coating the heels of Jack's boots in dust.

They positioned themselves around the door, Neave rocking on the balls of her feet, Winn clipping and unclipping tools on her toolbelt. Jack held his breath until the door finally skated sideways, revealing a tousle of dark brown hair and Jame's grinning face centered in a slice of orange light.

"Been long enough," Jame said. The tip of his nose was smudged with soot, but his face glowed with excitement. "We hit a few snags. The door was locked with a Thieflock. Nalissa might be still ... Give me a second, I'm going to check on her."

He jogged back through the mill, and Neave slid the door open wider, admitting them into the building. Jack stepped over the threshold and blinked. The space was strange to him at night. A nimbus of orange light encircled a nearby vat of churning Adrudian, but in every other direction, the mill was dark as the shore outside. Empty aisles and the silent bulks of machines stood out from the shadows.

"Is something ... burning?" Neave asked, closing the door behind them. She rubbed smoke out of her eyes. The surrounding haze had filled Jack's nostrils, too, stinging his sinuses.

"Not burning, just running." Jame appeared on the iron platform skirting the glowing vat. "Nalissa turned on this big wheel thing. It smoked a bit. She's not here, but we found the panel upstairs. She must have gone to shut off the power."

Jack shaded his eyes, watching the machine's huge metal shovels as they combed through the shaking vat. No wonder the rumbling had been familiar.

"She won't be able to turn it off upstairs—it has its own engine," Jack said. "It's called a turnover machine. The shovels stir the cooking Adrudian." His days working at the mill were spent standing at the edge of that vat, shoveling Adrudian over a tray and into a shipping container.

Jame kicked coppery liquid from the sole of his boot. "Turns out it kills clockworks, too. Genius move on Nalissa's part, really." He bade them toward the turnover machine. "Come see."

Winn held back, pushing a pair of goggles onto her forehead. She turned to Cameron. "Go with the others. Keep in sight of the door. I have a lift to open."

Cameron gave her a warm smile. "Be careful," he said, sounding so untroubled it grated on Jack's ears.

"I'll go with the Princess," Neave said. She caught sight of Winn's expression and grinned, her pointy canines flashing. "What? I can make myself useful."

"Fine," Winn said, and they darted off down an aisle toward the gleaming door of the mine shaft.

Jack knew the path to the turnover machine well enough to walk it in his sleep. Even the shovel he used to haul ore during his workdays was leaning against the side of the vat where he had left it. Still, as he trailed Cameron up the steps, he made note of the unfamiliar: the iron platform skirting the Adrudian vat had been chewed up, evidence of some recent fight, and the turnover machine was lurching with an odd, staggering rhythm. Strangest of all, the severed legs of a clockwork guard were lying at the end of the platform, twitching in a spray of Adrudian Milk.

Cameron whistled. He crouched by the clockwork's jittering, squarish feet and poked one with a long finger. "What happened to the other guard?"

"No idea." Jame perched on the railing across from them. "But Nalissa got it out of the way. It's gone."

Jack strode past Cameron and peered through the bars of the turnover machine. The clockwork's top half was curled beneath the spokes, crushed into Milk-soaked chunks. Curious, he pressed the button on the control box. The button clicked, but the machine's shovels continued to move. The mechanism was broken. Without an off switch, the turnover machine would rotate until its engine ran out of Adrudian power.

There goes my job.

"Unusual, but ... effective," Cameron said, shoving the clockwork's legs to the edge of the platform.

"I'll go upstairs and find her." Jame shifted his legs over the railing, making to drop to the floor below. "Did you know she's afraid of heights?"

Cameron frowned, surprised. "A Quandary Thief? Afraid of heights?"

"Yeah," Jame replied, his expression thoughtful. "That's a first."

Jack kneeled at the lip of the vat and sank his hand into the swirling rocks. The ore was warm. Not hot enough to burn, but it was only a matter of time. With the turnover machine broken, by morning the vat would be a sloshing pool of Adrudian Milk.

Jame cast a glance behind him. "By the way, the mill warden is here."

Jack's head shot up.

"The *what* is here?" Cameron said.

"The mill warden." Jame extended his hand, referring to a height at Jack's chest. "About this high. Yellow hair. Pretty strong for someone so deep in a whiskey bottle."

"Rhody Charlotte." Jack lifted his gaze to the north wall. The office window stared from above like a single, spying eye. He shuddered. Rhody Charlotte had given him a job, but that was where her kindness ended. She spent half of her time drinking in her office and the other half harassing her mill workers.

"She's stuck up there, for now." Jame fished in his

pocket, then dangled a ring of keys between his index finger and thumb. "I locked her in her office while Nalissa dealt with the clockworks."

Jack took the keys, suddenly nauseous. Rhody Charlotte's secrets were only as good as a few coins. If she so much as opened her mouth, their expedition was undone.

His knowledge imparted, Jame swung over the railing and jogged down the mill's main aisle, calling Nalissa's name. Jack and Cameron watched him disappear into the shadows.

"It's the middle of the night," Cameron said. He swept a hand over his jaw as Jack pocketed the keys, iron sitting cold against his hip. "Does Rhody Charlotte often work late?"

Jack scanned the lit window on the opposite wall. The room appeared empty. He imagined Rhody Charlotte burrowing herself into stacks of paper, rat-like. "How should I know if she works late?"

"You and Rhody Charlotte drink together after work. Neave told me."

Great. Jack pressed his lips into a line. Neave and Cameron had been talking about him. The notion was unpleasant. Almost as unpleasant as drinking with Rhody Charlotte had been.

"Only once, to get information about the mines," he said gruffly. After a beat, he added, "I don't think she works late."

"She knew we were coming, then. The Thieflock. She tried to protect the mill."

Jack stared at the clockwork's severed legs. They jerked like a pair of dying fish, coated with brass-orange slime. "Rhody Charlotte's not the protective type. Someone would have paid her."

"Perfect." Cameron took a deep breath, releasing it through pursed lips. "We'll have to persuade her to tell us who it was."

Jack let out a dry laugh. "How do you plan to do that?"

"Gold. *Someone* bought out my brandy stores last night." Cameron smiled his celebrity smile, eyes sparkling. His hand dove into his pocket and returned with four shiny gold pieces, the same pieces Jack had left on the bar in the Harper and Cup.

A moment passed before Jack could think of a response. The casual mention of the brandy had thrown him, as had the smile. "It'll take more than four gold pieces to convince Rhody Charlotte," he said finally. "She doesn't like Watch. Especially not Head Watch. And you shouldn't be showing her your face at all."

"Who said I was doing the convincing?"

They stared at each other, Cameron grinning as if he could persuade Jack to do his bidding through sheer charm. Jack's jaw pinched.

"Just give me the gold," he said, and held out his palm. His job was already lost, and Rhody Charlotte knew he was good for a bribe.

Cameron's hand disappeared into his pocket again, depositing the coins back into the folds of his jacket. "You can't get rid of me that easily. We're on a team now." He smiled again, but softer this time. "I'll come with you. She doesn't have to see either of us through the window."

Jack dug his elbows into his sides. He preferred not to think of himself as on the team at all. Plus, the idea of being alone with Cameron for an extended period made his stomach dance, a peculiar combination of annoyance and anticipation.

"I can do it myself," he said.

Cameron waved a hand. "I know, but that's what a team is for." He shot Jack a knowing look. "And anyway, I've been thinking about what you said last night."

Jack drew a short breath. He didn't want to talk about last night—but he did. He stood motionless, watching Cameron trace the railing with his fingertip. "Which part?"

"Some secrets shouldn't stay secret."

The flask in Jack's pocket grew heavy. He touched the metal through his jacket, recalling the expression Cameron had given him: panicked, fearful. Had he changed his mind? Had he been the one to burn the Adrudian in the lantern after all?

Jack shook his head. "Like you said ... the memory of the expedition is gone, but it isn't meant to be gone."

"Right," Cameron replied. He leaned against the railing and tipped his head back to examine the ceiling.

"But I'm not talking about what happened in the Shute. That can wait. I'm talking about the reason I asked you to come with us in the first place."

Behind him, the Adrudian churned, drawing in and out like the tide. Jack's hand fell from the flask. He had wondered countless times why Cameron had asked him here, but now that he was about to find out, he wasn't sure he wanted to know. His chest squeezed. He offered a mindless response.

"Because I—I have the map."

Cameron laughed, a gentler sound than his usual chuckle. "No, not the map." He gestured to the sides of Jack's cheeks. "Because of those."

The veins. Jack made an effort to keep his hands from covering his face.

"You shouldn't have to deal with that alone," Cameron said, still studying the rafters. His neck cut a clean line from his jaw, then plunged into his collar, after which Jack looked pointedly away. "Drinking Adrudian, your visions, the House of Matchsticks ...you can share those secrets, if you want. Give and take." His gaze flicked down to Jack. "That goes for me, too."

Jack folded his arms. "What are you saying?"

"I'm saying that I owe you." Cameron pushed from the railing, taking a tiny step forward. "You told me about your visions last night. Which means ... I owe you a secret."

The rumbling from the turnover machine muffled. Jack pressed his fingers into his forearm. What secrets could Cameron have? Secrets that didn't need to be squeezed with exhaustion, or the late night, or brandy—secrets willingly shared?

Jack swallowed a burning that had appeared in his throat. He said, "You don't have to tell me anything."

"I want to." Cameron's voice lowered, barely audible beneath the tumbling Adrudian. "And we're running out of time, so ..."

He held out his hand, as if for a handshake. Jack looked at it, frozen, rendered mute.

"I don't want to be rivals anymore," Cameron said. "That's my secret. That's why I asked you to come. I want you as my ally. Or friend." He paused, giving a barely perceptible shrug. "Or something."

Jack stared at the outstretched hand. His body had gone still, but his mind whirled, trying to parse Cameron's words until they made sense.

"If you have any more visions," Cameron said, "you can tell me. Not because you have to, but because you can." His hand reached further, lessening the space between them. "I'm asking you to."

Jack opened his mouth, then closed it again. Cameron was drawing a line. Not between them, as Jack would have suspected, but connecting them. One to the other. A stronger truce than a flask of night-old Adrudian would have been. He wanted to be friends.

Who am I to Cameron Agustin? Jack thought, not for

the first time, but the question had abruptly sharpened. A sudden knifepoint.

The seconds stretched. Cameron's hand hovered. Jack made to move—some movement, any movement—but then Jame came running around the side of the Adrudian vat, interrupting them with a waving arm.

Jack and Cameron turned. Jame skidded to a stop, out of breath, face pale as paper. In one hand, he clutched the long bar of Nalissa's collapsed trident. In the other, her backpack, smeared with grime.

"I can't find Nalissa," he said, eyes glassy in the orange glow. He steadied himself against the Adrudian vat. "She's gone."

Jame's information popped the bubble forming around Jack and Cameron. The three of them exchanged looks, the situation sinking in. Nalissa was missing.

Cameron sprang into motion, flying down the steps. Jack took a second to unlock his legs and followed. Ahead of them, Jame slipped around the Adrudian vat and ran back through the mill, holding the trident above his head like a flag.

"Nalissa!" he called, voice echoing through the machines. "Where are you?"

"Rhody Charlotte." Cameron gave Jack a sidelong look as they cut a course down the main aisle. He seemed to have forgotten about his unshaken hand, at least for now. "She could have seen something."

"From her office?" Jack said, though he privately agreed. If anything had happened to Nalissa, Rhody Charlotte could have spotted it through the window. His shoulders tightened. "I'll meet you there."

Cameron sidled around the slumped body of a clockwork pickaxer, vanishing into the dimness while Jack changed direction and headed east. The last few minutes had been dreamlike. Strange as one of his visions. Was he really here, breaking into the mines with Cameron—Cameron who wanted to be his friend? And was Nalissa really gone?

The space between his eyes ached.

Think. He stepped over a discarded piece of pipe, moving as quickly as he could through the dark. *Focus on Nalissa.*

She had been jittery before they'd boarded the ferry. Jack had seen as much: Her standing at the dock with the keyhole pendant clutched in her hand. Afraid. But afraid enough to desert them?

No. Think, Jack. She couldn't have. This was an island. Save for the death wish of rowing to Lower Village in the freezing night, Nalissa didn't have the means to leave. And she wouldn't abandon her trident.

He sidestepped a conveyor belt and emerged before the burnished door to the mine shaft. Winn and Neave had set up their flashlights to illuminate the small, wheelbarrow-scuffed space. The shiny surface of the door reflected the light, bouncing orange from side to side.

"That's not going to work," Winn was saying.

Neave was busy running her fingers down the slice in the middle of the door, tugging on each side to try to force it open. Next to her, Winn kneeled before the control box, its smooth metal cover lying at her feet. Jack caught the flash of a silver needle as she poked it through a nest of metal and gears.

Neave rubbed her palms. "You might have fancy tools, Princess, but sometimes all that's needed is a little—*eeuu-urgh.*" She pressed her fingertips into the door's middle and pulled hard to the side. The door didn't budge. Groaning, she shook out her hands. "Stupid thing."

"Hold this." Winn held out the needle. With her other hand, she unclipped a wrench. "You wanted to help."

"So I did." Neave took the needle with a good-natured huff and rested one shoulder against the door. She looked up as Jack entered their space, boots kicking up dust. "There he is! You couldn't find a way to shut off that wheel thing?" She jiggled an earlobe. "It'll knock my eardrums loose soon."

Jack came to a stop at the edge of the light. "The girl's missing."

"Missing?" Neave peered through her lashes at something beyond Jack's shoulder. "Is that her upstairs? Someone's making a racket up there."

He followed her gaze to the north wall. Cameron was

just visible, his weapons belt gleaming as he ascended the stairs. His footsteps were drowned out by a loud banging coming from the office door.

"That's not Nalissa," Jack said, wincing at the sound. "It's the mill warden. She stayed the night."

Neave's shoulder slid out from under her. She righted herself with a hand against the wall. "The warden knew we were coming?"

"Could be."

A gear rotated inside the control box with a rapid *click-click-click*. Winn tinkered around it with a tiny pair of pliers, her back hunched. "Find Nalissa quick," she said. "Once I get the door open, it won't stay that way for long. If she's not here to take the lift ... I don't want her to get left behind."

Neave cast her eyes over the bare aisles, painted lips dropping into a frown. No doubt she was thinking the same as Jack: there was no way for a girl, even a Thief, to get off a rock island in the space of twenty minutes.

"She's got to be in the mill somewhere." Neave pushed her sleeves to her elbows. "I'll look around."

Winn took back the silver needle, brushing a bead of sweat from her upper lip. She glanced at Jack. "Pay the warden if you have to. Find out who asked her to stay."

Jack bridled at the instruction, but he bit his tongue and strode to the north wall. Halfway up the staircase, Cameron stood with his back pressed against the closed office door. He was glowering, skin shining apricot in the window's orange glow. The thumping sound grew louder as Jack mounted the stairs.

"She's not happy," Cameron said.

"Bastard!" came Rhody Charlotte's voice from inside the office. "Let me see your face!"

A torrent of curses was followed by three hard whacks against the door. Cameron's body bounced. He jabbed a hand toward the window, inviting Jack to look.

Jack backtracked two steps and peered through the glass. The office was destroyed: ripped, yellowing papers layered the floor in stacks; the chairs had been broken and tipped on their sides; even the wooden desk had been pushed up against the wall, teetering precariously on two legs.

In the corner of the room, wrenching at the doorknob with both hands, was Rhody Charlotte. Her wild, rat-chewed hair bobbed around her face like a gaseous cloud, obscuring her beady eyes. She was pulling at the door with so much force her toes were off the ground, heels dug hard into the floor.

"Unlock this door!" she demanded, shouldering a spot of saliva from the corner of her mouth. "Give me my keys!"

Jack rapped his knuckle on the window. Rhody Charlotte's head whipped in his direction, and their eyes met with a painful slowness. For a second, Jack thought she didn't recognize him, but then her mouth flattened to a slit, a scrunched arrow appearing between her brows. She abandoned the door and pressed a grimy finger to the windowpane.

"*You*," she said, giving him a look of perfect hatred. "Should have known it was you."

Jack didn't know how to respond, so he cringed and held out his hands, an awkward apology. Cameron snorted.

Rhody Charlotte smacked the glass with the heel of her hand. "Who do you have on the other side of this door, Blueveins?" She backed up and booted the door, making Cameron's legs jolt. "Is it that little Thief boy?"

Jame. She'd seen him, which meant she could have seen Nalissa, too.

"Listen to me," Jack said, raising his voice to be heard through the glass. Rhody Charlotte returned to the window, watching him with narrowed eyes. "Did you see a girl here?"

"*Let me out!*" Each word was punctuated with a tight-fisted slam against the window. She pressed her snub nose to the glass. "Your secrets aren't so secret, Blueveins. A nice, white-gloved Watchman told me to expect intruders tonight. Gave me a bottle for my trouble."

"Donborough," Jack murmured. He and Cameron looked at each other. How did Donborough know about their expedition—and how had he gotten Rhody Charlotte to accept a gift from him? A bribe from Jack was one thing, but she despised all members of the Watch. The man clearly knew how to sweet talk.

"Donborough, yes, that was his name." Rhody Charlotte's breath puffed rounds of fog on the windowpane. "You know him. Figures. You're always in bed with Watchmen."

A beat passed, then Cameron arched an eyebrow. "*Are* you?"

"What? No," Jack said quickly. He waved away Cameron's smirk and turned to Rhody Charlotte. "We'll pay you."

Rhody Charlotte's face went from red to purple, her cheeks bulging, but she didn't reply. Jack held out a hand to Cameron, who dropped the four gold pieces into his palm. He pressed his hand to the window.

"Tell us." Jack leaned into his hand, pushing each coin flat against the glass. "Have you seen a Thief girl? With brown hair?"

Rhody Charlotte's gaze snagged on the gold, then lifted to Jack's face. She was so short she had to crane to look him in the eye. "I saw her."

Jack's heart drummed. He drew close to the glass. "Where is she?"

"Saw it from the window." To his surprise, Rhody Charlotte's face stretched into a grin, showing her skull's every tooth. "Quite a spectacle. Let me out, Blueveins, and I'll tell you exactly what happened."

A shiver crawled up Jack's arms. There was something unsettling about her smile, a cunning that went beyond

Rhody Charlotte's usual schemes. He looked at Cameron, whose face had taken on the color of chalk.

"Come on. She's got to be hurt," Cameron whispered.

Jack swore under his breath. He didn't want to give in, but Cameron was right. There wasn't a choice. His visions meant nothing without Nalissa. If they couldn't find her, the House of Matchsticks would slip from his grasp before he'd even closed his fingers.

He thrust his hand into his pocket and dug out the keys.

"Tell the others." Jack nudged Cameron aside and bent over the lock, dividing the office key from the rest of the ring. "I'll deal with Rhody Charlotte."

Cameron gave him an appraising look. "Be careful," he said, and this time he sounded like he meant it. He thumbed open his flashlight and hurried down the stairs.

Jack took a second to watch the orange cone of his flashlight shrink into the distance. He slid the office key into the lock.

"I've figured it out, you know," Rhody Charlotte said. She coughed as Jack turned the key. "That was the Head Inspector. Your City Watch boyfriend."

Jack barked a laugh. "Not my boyfriend."

"You've always been stupid, Blueveins." Rhody Charlotte' appeared in the doorway, digging her thumb into the side of her neck, scraping some unknown smudge. "But you can't be *that* stupid."

Jack ignored the barb and stepped back, pressing

himself against the staircase's railing, giving her a free path down the stairs. Rhody Charlotte stayed put, regarding him with thinned lips. He sighed and held out the gold.

"Tell me where the girl is."

Rhody Charlotte stowed the coins in her apron and shuffled toward him. Her hair was a tangled curtain framing her face.

"The funny thing is," she said, her glossy eyes flashing, "that girl's dead."

Jack furrowed his brow. The words melted into his brain like hot wax. Nalissa, dead? *No.* Rhody Charlotte was lying. She had to be.

"Tell the truth."

Rhody Charlotte's teeth gleamed, butter-yellow in her red gums. "I am. Your little Thief girl rode that turnover machine a-a-all—" She drew out the word, circling her fingertip through the air. "—all the way into the Adrudian."

She pointed at the ground.

The Adrudian vat. Jack's body went cold.

"I'll tell you why it's funny, Blueveins." Rhody Charlotte took another step closer. "When they dredge her body out of the Milk tomorrow, that girl will be ..." She skimmed a fingertip down the side of his cheek. "Just like you."

Jack's lungs shriveled. *The Adrudian vat. Nalissa was buried in the Adrudian vat.* If she'd fallen in recently, she might still be just beneath the surface—and the ore was light enough not to crush her—but he needed to get there before she suffocated, or the ore turned into Milk, or both.

Rhody Charlotte leered at him, enjoying the realization passing over his face.

"Sorry, Blueveins." She said it deep in her throat. A threat. "You and your friends will be dead before you can get there."

It happened too quickly for Jack to react. Rhody Charlotte snarled, flung herself forward, and shoved him on the chest. Jack had a fraction of a second to recognize what she'd done—Rhody Charlotte was killing him, really *murdering* him—before he fell over the railing backward.

The mill flipped, a black-orange coin. Jack's guts rolled as he pitched into the air. He fell for a split-second, a gasp escaping his mouth, before he managed to seize an iron bar lining the underside of the stairs. His shoulders jolted in their sockets, his palms squeaked, but he caught himself. He didn't let go.

Silence descended. The mill stretched before and below him, a sea of murky machines. Jack's chest heaved. He was dangling from the staircase with twisted wrists, his arms trembling.

Rhody Charlotte had tried to *kill* him.

The thought sent a dark feeling through his chest, a cocktail of shock and fury. He craned to look through the grate. On the stairs above, Rhody Charlotte's boots thumped to the railing, where she rested her elbows. Jack's throat constricted, but she wasn't looking for him. She was gazing over the rest of the mill, to where Jack imagined she could see the tiny figures of Winn, Neave, Jame, and Cameron.

The thin bar pressed the skin of Jack's fingertips to putty. He bit back a groan. He couldn't hang here forever. Shifting, ignoring the agony in his hands, he watched Rhody Charlotte lean over the railing and draw a long inhale, chest expanding beneath her too-big mill worker's top.

You and your friends will be dead before you can do anything, she had said.

Your friends.

The fire in Jack's arms suddenly drained, replaced by a numb dread. It had been stupid, letting Rhody Charlotte out. He knew what she was going to do. What she had been planning to do all along.

"Stop ..." he rasped, struggling against his knotted wrists, but for the second time in half-a-minute, Jack was too late.

"Intruders in the mines!" Rhody Charlotte bellowed. Her voice echoed through the quiet mill, bouncing off wood and iron and brick. The figures of Cameron, Neave, Winn, and Jame stilled—could he really see them, or was he imagining it?—and stared up at the north wall.

Intruders in the mines. Jack let off a little moan. They couldn't be just words, could they? They had to be words said in the right way, by the right voice, in the right order.

Intruders in the mines was an activation phrase.

A spot of orange light materialized, winking into being from within the darkness of the mill, about the size of a dinner plate. Then another spot appeared, followed by another, and another. The mill's floorspace was a blanket of orange lights, numbers beyond Jack would ever have guessed. Twenty, or more.

The orange bellies raised themselves, puppets pulled on strings. Standing. Stretching. The fine points of their pickaxes catching the light, glistening.

A strangled cry came from within the forest of machines. The voice sounded like Neave, but it could have been Winn, or Jame. Or Cameron. Any of them. A pickaxe collided with metal. Something overturned, crashing.

Above him, Rhody Charlotte backed into her office and slammed the door, locking it from the inside. Rage sparked inside Jack, turning his vision a beating red. She was going to cower inside her office while they were slaughtered.

"Winn," a voice shouted. This time it was definitely Neave. A wheelbarrow skidded across the floor, sent spinning by the flat of some giant wooden foot. "Hurry up and open that door, please."

"I'm trying." Winn sounded hoarse. Jack could just see her figure bowed before the control box. Two, three, four orange lights were headed her way, weaving through the dark. "Thirty seconds!"

Thirty seconds. Too short to dig Nalissa out of the vat.

Too long to destroy twenty clockwork pickaxers on their own. Jack's hands quaked. His little finger slipped from its hold, a deep red groove where the bar had been biting into his skin.

"Jack, let go!"

He jerked, startled. The words had come from the pool of blackness below him. Panting, he swung his head side-to-side.

"Where are ..." Jack couldn't get the last word out.

"I'm beneath you, you idiot," Cameron said. He was out of breath, sentence escaping between gasps. "Let go."

He looked down. The space beneath his feet seemed endless, a void waiting to consume him. But his grip was loosening, his heart thrashing, and there was no time left. Jack did as he was told, and let go, and fell into space.

He landed hard on a soft surface. Cameron had wheeled a giant bin of rags beneath him. The milk-encrusted fabric broke his fall, but the impact still jarred his legs. He crumpled to his hands and knees, wheezing.

"Graceful, that," Cameron said, the corner of his mouth quirking. He held out a hand to help Jack from the bin, but Jack ignored it and gestured toward the mill's main aisle.

"Nalissa ..." He gasped a breath, hanging his head. "She's buried in ... the Adrudian vat."

A moment of silence, then Cameron said, "Is she dead?"

"I don't know. Go ... go. And turn on as many machines as you can." Rhody had activated the clockworks to attack, but pickaxers didn't have the same senses as guards—the extra movement and noise might confuse them. It was a long shot, but the only chance they had. "Go. I'll follow you."

"Stars," Cameron said, and sprinted off toward the turnover machine, hair winking in the dim amber light.

Jack tested a wrist, an ankle. Fire licked at his muscles, but nothing seemed to be broken. That was good. A machine tipped somewhere in the darkness, smashing against the floor. Behind the banging metal was the thud of clockwork legs coming in his direction. He stood shakily.

Walk.

One step through the rags. His legs didn't wobble. His knees held. A circle of orange light appeared around the side of a furnace, its bearer so tall the dark swallowed its misshapen, faceless head.

Run.

Jack scrambled free of the bin as the clockwork lunged. A pickaxe the length of his arm whizzed through the air, missing him by a breath. His heart hammered. No time to hesitate. No time to think.

He bolted down the aisle after Cameron, skirting empty wheelbarrows, leaping over scattered Adrudian, stumbling once, twice, three times over the uneven floor. He hit buttons with his fist as he went, conveyor belts erupting to life, furnaces coming aglow. A pickaxer loping behind him hacked at the rotating arm of a grinder. Jack kept running. There were only so many machines in the mill that could catch the clockworks' attention. He trained all his focus on the wheel.

Ahead, a second clockwork barreled through the arms of a spindly sorting machine, straight into his path. Jack's breath disappeared. He ducked, throwing himself to the filthy floor to avoid the arc of the clockwork's shining pickaxe. The point dented the furnace behind him with a brain-shaking *clang*. A nearby group of hanging ropes rippled.

Jack scrambled across the ground on his stomach, then turned and unsheathed his dagger. There was a shadow above—a crate hanging from a pulley. The clockwork advanced on him, pickaxe raised. Panting, Jack grabbed the nearest rope and sawed through the fibers. *Snap*. He threw himself out of the way as the crate came crashing to the ground, pinning the clockwork beneath a wave of iron scraps and splintered wood.

Then he was up and running again, sliding his dagger back into its sheath.

Halfway there. A little more.

He passed the intersection that opened onto the mine shaft doors. Winn was on her feet, bent over the control box, using a tiny screwdriver to attach the metal cover back to the wall. Neave and Jame were on either side of her, Jame fending off a pickaxer with a wheelbarrow while Neave brandished a torn piece of pipe like a bat.

"Is that really necessary?" Neave said to Winn as Jack streaked past, slipping on the dirt-strewn concrete.

Winn fitted another screw to the head of the screwdriver. Her hands were trembling. "For the Spider I installed to work, yes," she said. "Just give me ten seconds ... ten seconds ..."

Jack left them behind. He rounded a bend and the turnover machine rose like a tower. A fresh wave of energy rolled through him. Cameron was already there, kneeling on the iron platform, his face reddened as he shoved the edge of the vat. Trying to tip it over.

But before Jack got close enough to help, a clockwork pickaxer clambered up onto the platform behind Cameron. When Cameron turned to look, his arms slipping from the edge of the vat, his sleeves were soaked with brassy Adrudian Milk.

"No," Jack breathed. A shock went through him, from the clockwork or the Milk he didn't know. He sprinted toward the platform. The shovel leaning against the vat had tipped and was lying diagonally on the concrete; he scooped it from the floor and pounded up the steps, legs numb, mind blank. The clockwork pulled itself over the railing, bearing down on Cameron.

Jack shoved the blade into its glowing middle.

The clockwork, taken off guard, swung its pickaxe and

stumbled backward. A crack had opened in its wooden belly. Jack released the shovel and hurled himself out of the way as the clockwork fell back onto the wheel machine. There was a tremendous *crunch* as its head wedged between two shivering bars. The iron spokes groaned and stalled.

"Two seconds!" Winn's voice yelled above the tumult.

"Move over," Jack said to Cameron, who looked stunned, blinking as if Jack had flown in on a dragon. "We'll push together on three. I'll find Nalissa—the Milk can't hurt me."

Cameron wrapped a hand around the edge of the vat. "You *stabbed* that thing," he said.

"I know," Jack muttered. "Now push."

He counted to three. He and Cameron held their breath and shoved the Adrudian vat with all their strength. The metal was heavy, but with the turnover machine jammed, the vat uncoupled from its base and rocked outward. Jack pushed harder as rocks clattered over the far side, and then the whole vat was tipping over, sending a wave of orange avalanching across the concrete floor. It landed with a crash, shaking Jack's teeth in his head.

"Nalissa," Cameron said.

Jack didn't need the reminder. He leaped over the side of the overturned vat and into the heap of Adrudian beyond. He dug through the airy rocks, sharp edges cutting into his knuckles, pulse pounding in his throat.

The chalky liquid had slopped everywhere. What if Nalissa had drowned, like Rhody Charlotte said? An innocent girl would die, and the House of Matchsticks would never be found, and it would all be for nothing.

"Now!" It was Winn.

A mechanical *whoosh* sounded. Out of the corner of his eye, Jack saw the mine shaft door slide open. The pickaxers had reduced the machines between the door and the vat to scrap metal, providing a clear view. Beyond the mine shaft door was a tiny space, a cool metal room, with a single Adrudian bulb hanging from a string.

The lift.

Winn ran inside and kneeled by the wall, poking at the patch of knobs and switches that controlled the mechanism. "The doors are going to close," she yelled. She frantically passed her hands over the wall. "I don't think I can stop them."

Jack's arms seized.

"What if she's not in the Adrudian?" Cameron said. His voice was shaking, watching Neave swing her iron pipe at a clockwork's glowing waist. "What if Rhody Charlotte lied?"

The words entered Jack's ears but bounced away unnoticed. His fingers had caught something inside the pile. A handful of slippery fabric. The back of a Casret Academy-issue blazer.

Whump. The side of the vat rocked. Jack cast a wide-eyed glance to his left, his blood going cold. A clockwork guard had unearthed itself from the Adrudian heap beside him. Ore clattered and tumbled as it crawled over the vat's edge, headed for the iron platform. Its massive, swinging head ignored Jack and went straight for Cameron, who drew his Watchman's dagger from his belt.

"Guess we found the second guard," he said, twirling his knife in his fingers.

As they started to fight, Jack tore his eyes away and reached further into the Adrudian. He grasped Nalissa's blazer in one hand and dug around her with the other. A curl of Milk-soaked hair appeared. Behind him, Cameron danced away from the clockwork's sword, a stream of blood dripping from his upper arm.

Rocks clattered. Nalissa's head emerged from the Adrudian, her neck slack. Jack let out a choked breath. Her face was clear—no blue veins—but she was drenched in Adrudian Milk. It dripped from her lips. She was unconscious. If she opened her mouth...

With renewed energy, Jack dug through the Adrudian and hauled her upward. The rest of her limp body appeared, soaked bronze and dripping. Her chin lolled on her chest.

Jack cast a quick glance across the mill. Neave was fighting off pickaxers while Jame braced himself inside the door to the lift. The doors were trying to close, but he was holding them open on either side, arms shuddering. Winn was just visible behind him, pressing buttons in a panic.

Hurry.

He slung Nalissa over one shoulder, his muscles quivering in pain and fatigue. On the platform, the clockwork attacking Cameron curved its arm in a quick strike. Its body was between them, so Jack couldn't see Cameron dodge, but he must have; the clockwork's sword embedded itself in the iron platform.

Maybe it was the shock, or the pain radiating through his shoulders, but it took Jack a moment to notice his front was slick, wetness cooling his chest, neck, and chin. A rivulet of brassy liquid was slipping down the side of his face, flowing from Nalissa's soaked clothes. Stinging his eye. Dripping onto his mouth.

Into his mouth.

Jack coughed. His tongue was bitter, chalky. He swallowed reflexively and the taste spread, rolling down his throat. A pang of horror turned his stomach—or was that the Adrudian Milk, burning his chest, seeping into his veins, a chemical hand with flexing fingers reaching to pull a vision over his eyes?

Jack's world veered. The clockwork wrenched at its sword, mere seconds from yanking it free. Where Cameron had been there was now an empty space; he'd escaped, heading toward the mine shaft with his bleeding arm clutched in one hand. No doubt he thought they had saved Nalissa. No doubt he thought they were safe.

Jack took a step, putting one foot in front of the other. His spine creaked. The vision was coming. He could feel it overtaking him, like he was falling backward into sleep.

He needed to get to the mine shaft.

Fighting the growing haze in his head, Jack stumbled down the Adrudian pile under Nalissa's weight and ran toward the lift. Both Jame and Neave were holding the doors open now, sheens of sweat coating their foreheads. The door emitted a roaring hiss.

Stay awake, he told himself, scrambling over the remnants of chopped-up machines. His mind barely registered that the mill had been razed, its floor a spread of broken metal. He fixed his eyes on the mine shaft. Closer, closer. Cameron had ducked inside, sliding between Neave and Jame.

There was a harsh *clank* behind him: the clockwork wresting its sword free of the platform. Jack lurched around a wheelbarrow on dead legs. More clockworks would be coming. Following. His tongue numbed in his mouth. Nalissa's arms dangled over his shoulder.

Stay awake. The mine shaft was near, but the space between Jack and the door seemed to be stretching. The thud of clockwork feet echoed in his ears. His ankles trembled. The pickaxers were going to tear him apart while he was helpless, deep in an Adrudian vision.

Ahead, Winn abandoned the knobs and switches and extended her arms through the door, gesturing wildly with her hands.

"*Come on come on come on come on come on,*" she screamed.

Stay awake. But a haze was descending over Jack. His

senses weakened. A clockwork came up behind him and drew its pickaxe up and back, readying a death blow.

Bring the girl into the mines. Find the House of Matchsticks. Uncover the memory.

The resting period was over.

Jack staggered into the mine shaft, clutching Nalissa. He collapsed and landed in a tumble of arms and legs. Behind him, the two sides of the door clapped together with a *bang*. The clockwork's pickaxe hit the other side hard enough to dent the metal.

A shudder of impact, the Adrudian bulb on its string, and the feeling of cold hands at the back of his head. Then Jack was gone

gone

gone.

IT WASN'T DARKNESS, *this time. It was sunlight, glinting off the serrated leaves of musclewood trees, casting shadows over the dirt on his boots, warming the nape of his neck. The light wouldn't last, but Jack had come prepared with a pouch of extra Adrudian. He always began expeditions in the late afternoon.*

The entrance to the Shute was an inconspicuous break between trees. The spot would be easily missed if it were not marked by the Dead Tree, a giant, blackened oak with strange, leafless branches. He pressed two fingers to the brittle trunk, as he did at the start of all his expeditions. It was a lucky charm for the superstitious, but a formality for Jack.

His map unfolded in his hand, his constellation of clues that would lead him through the forest. There was the Dead Tree, in the northwest corner. At the bottom, marked with an X, was the House of Matchsticks. He saw his fingertip poking out of a worn leather glove, brushing the X. His feet crunched through dead leaves.

The vision shifted.

He was standing at the edge of a ravine, watching the rush of a little stream. Clear water skated over the tightly packed streambed. Jack swept his flashlight to the side. The forest was dark. He'd been walking for hours into the night.

Beneath the orange beam of his flashlight, the streambed sparkled a deep red-purple. In among the grayish rocks were hunks of gemstones, sharp chips, and fractures that glittered like ruby ink. A purpesia deposit.

Jack crouched at the edge of the ravine, looking closer. He edged his notebook out of his pocket and made a note. Purpesia was said to be cursed, but Jack didn't believe in curses. If he could find a path down into the ravine, he could carry a stone or two back to Ar.

As if hearing his thoughts, the ground beneath him suddenly shifted. Jack tried to stand, but the soil at the edge of the ravine broke loose. A spray of dirt fell twenty feet into the ravine, and Jack would have followed, if it hadn't been for a hand grasping his sleeve and pulling him hard back from the edge. Jack stumbled onto his backside, stunned and reaching for his dagger.

"Graceful, that," a familiar voice said.

Jack could hear the smile in it, on the border of a chuckle. He didn't bother to look up from the pair of pointed, polished boots that appeared by his side. He just buried his head in his hands, biting back a groan.

"What, not happy to see me?" Cameron unclipped a flashlight from his weapons belt and thumbed it open. A bright beam of Adrudian light slid across the grass, making the blades gleam. "Pretty sure I just saved your life."

Jack rose to his feet, his limbs heavy. "It's not that far a slide. I would have been fine."

Cameron strode carefully to the lip of the ravine, coming into full view. He was wearing a brown leather jacket with fleece on the collar, his hair sweeping tidily over his forehead.

"I wouldn't be so sure." Cameron peered into the ravine, rubbing at the back of his neck. "That's a lot of purpesia. Don't want to get cursed."

Jack looked meaningfully at him. "I already am."

Cameron laughed as if Jack were joking. He wasn't. Without another word, Jack set off through the forest, following the edge of the ravine. His stomach clenched. He had been sure to cover his tracks when he was doing research. How had Cameron found out about the expedition? How did Cameron find out about anything?

Jack savored the few seconds of silence before Cameron fell into step beside him.

"I assume you're looking for that ritual site," he said, edging around a tree root.

Frowning, Jack fixed his eyes on the stream below them. If he jumped in, what were the chances Cameron would follow? But Jack also didn't want to break his legs, so he just sighed and said, "The House of Matchsticks."

"Right." Cameron gave him an angled grin. "I'm looking for it, too."

Jack stopped walking. He glared at Cameron, at his wide smile and dark eyes. They had raced for countless artifacts over the years, but Cameron's habit of heading off the beginning of his expeditions was new. And he kept showing up alone, without his team. Why?

They stared at each other, Jack pressing a finger to one veinless cheek. The only explanation was that Cameron wanted to gloat. To show off how right *he was.*

Squaring his shoulders, Jack turned and climbed into the ravine, ignoring the slope's treacherous height. He clipped his shining flashlight to his belt, lowering himself over the edge, hands fisted into scrubby roots and dirt.

"Hey, wait," Cameron said, but Jack was already clambering down the side, toes rucked against the rocky edge.

He didn't slip, though the soil was shaky and loose. At the bottom, Jack jumped, splashing into the frigid streambed. Cameron said nothing as he waded down the ravine, headed in the same direction they had been walking.

Rocks of purpesia clattered around his feet. He swept his hand into the water, caught two of the deep red gemstones, and stowed them in his pocket.

For a time, Cameron walked silently along the ravine above. Then he climbed down into the stream, too, splashing his way through the water. The two of them traveled that way for the better part of thirty minutes, Jack stewing while Cameron picked his way through the stream behind him.

Eventually, Cameron's splashing footsteps stopped. Jack came to a halt, too. His numb feet had drained the anger from him, leaving only a dull annoyance. Sometime in the last half hour, he'd grown accustomed to the sound of Cameron trailing him. It offered a respite from the hushed forest, a silence that would have been peaceful anywhere but the Shute.

Jack turned, curving his flashlight over the stream. Cameron had crouched and was sifting through the water. He stood after a time, a glittering rock of purpesia in his hands. The stone was covered in silt, rough at the edges, and about the size of his thumb. Not worth much more than silver; the two rocks Jack had scooped up were shinier and better quality.

Cameron held the purpesia out so Jack could see it in the light. "Not bad," he said, shrugging.

His hands were glistening wet from the stream. A thought came unbidden to Jack: the water was freezing. His hands must be cold.

"Here." Jack pulled one of the two rocks of purpesia from his jacket. He tossed the larger one to Cameron, who caught it with a look of surprise. "This one's better."

Cameron examined it, a smile tugging at the corners of his mouth. After a moment, he said, "You're right."

In so many words, it was decided. They were stuck with each other.

Cameron dropped the purpesia in his pocket. Jack turned and continued into the inky darkness, his own purpesia stowed safely in his jacket. There was a strange feeling blooming inside him: the feeling of forgetting. Losing his mind. Losing his memory.

Losing the vision.

HE OPENED HIS EYES.

The shining Adrudian bulb swung back and forth, casting shadows long on the walls. Hearing came back by degrees: first an indistinct thrum, then a soft grinding sound, and finally a continuous, metallic growl. The floor was vibrating beneath him.

Jack groaned, shifting on his back. At the sound of his voice, someone shuffled near the wall, where the light didn't reach.

"He's awake," Winn said.

Neave's face appeared above him, blotting out the swaying bulb. She was pale and her makeup was smeared, but she flashed him a lupine grin. "Rise and shine. Been a while."

She retreated to the wall as Jack propped himself up on his elbows. His body was dense, limbs stony. The knuckles of his right hand ached where he had plunged them into the Adrudian. He stretched his fingers and was surprised to see a frayed bandage tied around his palm. It rattled him—he'd never had someone help him while he was in a vision.

Jack scraped a tangle of hair from his eyes. "Where are we?" he tried to ask, but his tongue was a wet bag in his mouth. He'd never had to talk so soon after a vision, either.

Winn seemed to understand his soupy words. "Right where we should be," she said. She was sitting in the corner, her tool belt jumbled around her hips, spinning a wrench between her fingers. The goggles she'd been wearing in the mill spilled out of a pouch on her belt. They'd left greasy marks around her eyes, cutting through her black brows.

"Speak for yourself, Princess," Neave said from the other wall. "How are we going to get back out of the mill again with those clockworks roaming around?"

Jack sat up, staring through the dim. *The lift.* He'd seen slices of it during his workdays but had never been inside. The space was so tiny there was barely enough room for him to be lying down in the center. Iron mesh bordered the walls, and beyond the mesh was rolling, rough stone, the deep architecture of the earth. They were descending into the mines.

To his left, Neave kneeled beside a slouching Cameron, winding a bandage around his bloodied arm. The sleeve of his button-down was pushed to his shoulder, his black jacket draped across his legs. Tired lines had appeared at the edges of his lips.

Jack opened his mouth to speak, but Cameron stopped him with a shake of his head.

"Not as bad as it looks," he said, wincing and smiling at once. He gestured behind Jack. "Good job with the rescue, by the way."

The memory of their escape flooded back. Jack whipped around, his heartbeat coming up, but Cameron was telling the truth: Nalissa was slumped against Jame's shoulder, her hair and clothes stiffened with Adrudian Milk. Someone had cleaned her face, removing the worst of the danger, and her eyes were closed. Her chest moved up and down with regular breath.

"She's asleep, I think," Jame whispered, fiddling with the rings on his index finger. Of them all, he appeared the most shaken, his hair sticking out at all angles.

Jack caught the glitter of crimson at the base of Nalissa's neck. The pendant was nested in her collar, its bronze chain crumpled. She'd kept from losing it—that was lucky. Its sparkle reminded him of rocks at the bottom of a shallow stream.

The wearer forgets.

The man-snake's voice surfaced in Jack's mind, making his skin prickle. Nalissa couldn't remember where she had gotten the pendant because *the wearer forgets.* Jack had dismissed the notion as unimportant, something the creature had said to pacify the King, but what if it wasn't? What if Nalissa had forgotten because the pendant was—

Something clanked, interrupting his thoughts. An old, rusted gate ascended into view. Jack's bones shook as the lift screeched to a halt. They had arrived at the bottom of the mine shaft.

Quiet descended over each of them. Jack squinted into the tunnel beyond the gate, but there was nothing. The dark was complete, a black wall, a pregnant emptiness hiding its face.

Neave tied the knot on Cameron's bandage, patted his arm, and got to her feet. Winn followed suit, then Cameron and Jack. Jame lifted a bleary Nalissa onto his back, tilting under her weight, then straightening with the rest of them.

A line of sweat trickled from Jack's brow. The air had grown warm, thick with the smell of Adrudian. It wasn't the chalky, bitter smell of processing Adrudian from the mill; this was the smell of raw Adrudian, earthy, wet, and old.

"What do you think," Jame said, breaking the silence, "sixteen odd years?"

"Since when?" Neave asked. She stepped closer to the

gate, reaching to run a fingertip along the deteriorated metal.

"Since anyone but a machine has been down here."

There was a long pause while they gazed into the darkness, each imagining the unseen passages that lay within.

"About that long, yes," Cameron said. His words were small in the hushed air.

No one seemed willing to move. After a minute, Winn edged to the front of the lift, unhooked the clasp on the gate, and drew it back. Its moan sliced through the quiet, echoing down whatever corridor stretched beyond. Winn waited for the echo to die, then turned to face the group of them. She'd strapped a pickaxer's headlamp to her forehead. Beneath the closed slats of the bulb, her eyes shone with both fear and determination.

"Whatever happens," she said, "we keep each other."

There was a round of silent agreement. Jack shifted from one foot to the other. He didn't know what she meant, to *keep* each other. The bandage on his hand pressed against his swollen knuckles. He didn't know what it meant to be kept.

Winn thumbed the dial on her headlamp, releasing a beam of sun-orange light. The tunnel yawned before them, rough rock on every side. Her headlamp could barely penetrate the darkness. Still, she took a step off the lift and strode into the mines. Neave followed, then Jame with Nalissa draped over his back. Their figures shifted to silhouettes, shrinking into the blackness.

Cameron lingered for a moment, fiddling with the strap of his headlamp. Then he squared his shoulders and moved to walk off the lift. Jack made a split-second decision.

"Wait." He reached to catch Cameron's arm, then paused, fingers hovering. Cameron turned. His eyes glinted in the dying light.

"Yes?"

"You asked me to tell you, so ... I'm telling you," Jack said. He took a deep breath, stale air filling his lungs. "It was the purpesia."

Cameron stared at him. "The purpesia?"

"It made us lose the memory. We took rocks of purpesia from the stream. That's the curse."

A complicated look crossed Cameron's face, something between wariness and surprise. Then his lips parted with a realization. "*The wearer forgets.*" He slipped a hand through his hair, shaking it out beneath the headlamp. "The curse is real."

"Could be."

Cameron nodded slowly. A patch of stubble beneath his chin tensed and released, then he said, "Thank you for telling me." He turned to head down the tunnel.

This time Jack caught him in earnest, his hand capturing his sleeve. Cameron stopped. He looked from Jack to his arm, and back again. His eyebrows rose.

"I wanted to ..." Jack started, but he hesitated. He had never understood who he and Cameron were to each other. Opponents, sure. Rivals, yes. But there was another part, too, something intrinsic he couldn't name. Something necessary to his existence, if Jack was honest, which he was beginning to think he never was. Not to himself.

He didn't know how to put all that into words, so he just held out his hand, as if for a handshake.

Cameron went still, staring at it. Then he broke into a wide smile. He grasped Jack's hand.

"Friends," he said.

"Something like that," Jack replied, in slight disbelief at his own words.

Cameron released his hand, leaving a tingling warmth behind. Jack stretched his fingers. *Something like that.*

Grinning at him, Cameron opened his headlamp and disappeared into the tunnel.

Jack stood still for a few seconds, counting his breaths. The *pull* strummed at his chest. He opened his backpack and pressed his headlamp to his forehead. The night had altered, fresh ink beneath his feet, but still the House of Matchsticks was waiting. He was drawing a map. A line between two points.

As he adjusted the strap on his headlamp, he had the distinct impression of something passing above his head. A puff of air. A fluttering sound.

He looked up, rolling his finger over the dial on his lamp. Orange light cascaded out, illuminating the tunnel's low rock ceiling. Empty, but he had the impression of a shadow at the corner of his eye. The sleek feathers of a bird's wing.

A bird, in a mine shaft?

"Jack," Neave's voice called from ahead. "Did you forget how to walk?"

"No, I'm coming," he replied.

Shaking his head, Jack pressed two fingers to the side of the tunnel. He tugged at his sleeves. He walked forward into the long dark.

THE ADVENTURE CONTINUES IN ...

PART THREE OF THE HOUSE OF MATCHSTICKS SERIES

Discover the next leg of the journey at elisadowning.com.

WANT FREE HOUSE OF MATCHSTICKS CONTENT?

Hi! Elisa here.

I hope you enjoyed *Night of Matchsticks* (Part 2). If you did, I'd love to hear from you in a review. Reviews help readers take notice of books—and even a sentence or two can mean the world to indie authors like myself. Thank you so much!

If you're itching to read more House of Matchsticks content, join my newsletter to receive your free House of Matchsticks Reader Bundle. You'll get a novelette starring Jack and Cameron, map downloads, and more. Find out more at my website: elisadowning.com.

As always, thank you for reading. And see you in the House of Matchsticks.

Elisa Downing

THE HOUSE OF MATCHSTICKS SERIES

House of Matchsticks
Night of Matchsticks
Tree of Matchsticks

ALSO BY ELISA DOWNING

Josie and the Scary Snapper

ABOUT THE AUTHOR

Elisa Downing is an author of strange stories about brave kids, teens, and new adults. An MA Children's Literature graduate, she's spent years climbing through the windows of books to better see the world beyond. She enjoys writing fantastical adventures full of ancient mysteries, slow-burn romance, and lots of monsters. When she's not writing, you can find Elisa reading under a tree somewhere, playing video games on easy mode, waxing poetic over cult cinema, or watching horror movies.

www.ingramcontent.com/pod-product-compliance
Lightning Source LLC
Chambersburg PA
CBHW030339310726
48979CB00001B/102

* 9 7 8 1 7 7 7 8 8 5 7 2 4 *